Naughty Stories from A to Z

Something dark, deep, and just a little bit scary was bubbling up inside me. I tossed my thong in my purse and threw on my black suede dress and pumps. Without bothering to put on panties, I grabbed my car keys and rushed out the back door. All I wanted was to get behind the wheel of my car and drive. A cherry-red '65 Vette is my priest, analyst, and best girlfriend all rolled into one. Any time something gets to me, I take it out on a lonesome highway in the dark and drive.

The faster the better.

Also by Alison Tyler:

The Blue Rose
The Virgin
Dial "L" for Loveless
Blue Sky Sideways and Other Stories
Venus Online
The Dark Room: An Online Adventure
Come Quickly: For Girls on the Go
The Silver Key
Batteries Not Included, ed.
Learning to Love It
Strictly Confidential
Sweet Thing
Sticky Fingers

Naughty Stories
from A to Z

Alison Tyler, editor

Novels published by
Pretty Things Press
contain sexual fantasies.
In real life, make sure you practice safe sex.

First Pretty Things Press Edition 2002

First Printing May 2002

ISBN 1-57612-168-2

Manufactured in the United States of America
Published by Pretty Things Press

10 9 8 7 6 5 4 3

The real fountain of youth is to have a dirty mind.
—Jerry Hall

for Sam
always

Contents

Introduction

All right, I'll admit it. I've always had a thing for the word 'naughty.' Call me a naughty girl and I'll blush and lose my poker face instantly. Deep down inside, I understand that there's something truly sexy about the word, something sly and knowing. And I am certainly not the only person who feels this way. You *know* when you're being naughty, and there is an impish delight, delectable and sweet, that makes behaving in a naughty fashion so much fucking fun.

That said, you'll have to understand how excited (read 'turned on') I was to riffle through the submissions for this naughty anthology. Because while my personal definition of being naughty is pretty well focused in my head, other writers have a whole world of different viewpoints of what that simple word encompasses. To me, naughty means pressing boundaries and breaking the rules. But others find that doing it on a plane, or outside, or (as in "Quiet, Quiet") in a lover's mother's bed equals being naughty. Some fetishes seem to lend themselves to 'naughty' themes—playing with feather dusters, making it with an ex-lover, dabbling in the art of erotic spanking. Sharing dirty secrets, as in "Trust Me," can be naughty, as can whispering filthy scenarios over a long-distance phone line (check out "X-rated Conversations").

But here's my real feeling—*you* are naughty, dear reader, simply for being drawn to an anthology with the word in the heading. You want to slip over to the darker side, away from the good girls and boys. You want to be on Santa's *other* list. I'm right, aren't I? And you're blushing now, too. So get ready for some naughty fun then, from some of the best erotic writers in the field.

Your Naughty Editor,

Alison Tyler

Appraising Love
by Dante Davidson

I have to admit it—and I hope this doesn't make me sound like a cad—but those legs were what caught my attention first. In all my years of searching, I'd never seen perfection like that. Delicately curved, almost achingly arched, they surpassed my wildest fantasies. I could imagine running my fingers up and around their smooth, supple surface for hours, getting down on my hands and knees to worship them. I've always been something of a leg man.

Slowly, I moved closer, feigning interest in the stature of several other, less lovely creations nearby. With extra effort, I maneuvered myself through the crowd, and when I was close enough, I reached out my hand, wanting just one touch....

"Hey!" a female voice said, sounding surprised. "What are you doing?"

"It's a—," I lowered my voice as I named the maker. "Isn't it?"

The owner raised her painted-on eyebrows, giving me a quizzical stare which I processed before returning my gaze to my newfound love. "How could you know that without checking the label?" she asked.

I didn't look at her while I answered. My eyes were still captivated by her table, those flawless legs, that haughty, aristocratic stance. The color was a rich, unmarred caramel that had obviously been untouched since it left the original creator's hands. Often, at such appraisal road shows, we see once-beautiful objects, now destroyed by an owner's idiotic—if well-intentioned—attempts at refinishing. *Never* mess with perfection.

Just to be entirely sure that the treasure was indeed as priceless as I thought, I got on my knees and crawled under the table. My heart pounded even faster as I read that golden label beneath the rim. There, in unblemished perfection, were the artisan's engraved initials. I smiled broadly when I saw them.

"Are you okay?" the owner asked. I had forgotten all about her until she bent down to peer at me under the table. Thinking back, I must have looked fairly ridiculous, dressed impeccably in my gray suit and navy blue tie, lying on the ground grinning up at the wood. The workmanship was remarkable, and I couldn't help but stroke the firm underside with the palms of my hands. If furniture could make a noise, this table would have purred.

"I'm fine," I said weakly, breaking free of my daze and looking at the owner's face. For the first time, I really noticed her. I took in her bright blue eyes and even brighter blue eye shadow. "I'm Jonathan Silver, appraiser for Winston-Logan."

Her attitude changed instantly, from "hands-off" to "help yourself."

"You work here," she said, indicating the breadth of the show with a sweeping glance. As I climbed out from under the table, I continued my brief observation of her face. She had two perfectly round circles of rouge on her cheeks making her appear as if she'd been playing dress up with her mother's cosmetics. Her lips sported an orange-coral shade not often found in nature. Once an appraiser, always an appraiser. It can be difficult to turn off the critical voice in my head.

"My name's Lucy," she said, offering me a hand, the nails of which were long and polished a vibrant, glistening green, like the underbelly scales of a tropical snake. When I let go of her hand, she ran it through her platinum teased hair, raising the height another inch or so with the gesture. What a woman like her was doing with a table like this, I could not imagine. But it's my job to judge furniture, not people, and I plastered a false smile on my face and turned on my professional charm.

"Will you go on air with it?" I asked.

Lucy gave an excited, high-pitched squeal, like a contestant on a game show. The noise was loud enough for our producer to hear, and when Corrine met my eyes from across the room, I nodded to indicate I had a winner. Oh, did I have a winner. Corrine rushed over and I whispered into her ear what I'd found.

"Are you sure, Jonathan?" Corrine asked incredulously, inspecting Lucy's attire, which did not exactly fit the normal type of clothes we see at the road show. Most people arrive in jeans and t-shirts, shorts if it's a hot day. The table's owner was wearing a revealing pink floral sundress loosely laced up the front. Part of my brain quickly categorized it as "cheap," and possibly "slutty." But another part of my brain — the one attached to a lower segment of my anatomy — understood how someone might find a dress like that appealing. The laces had come slightly undone in the front, and for some reason I envisioned myself taking a step closer and tying the bow for Lucy, my fingers brushing the skin of her supple breasts, touching her just as gently as only moments before I'd stroked the leg of her table.

At that thought, I found myself looking down at Lucy's own legs. Clad in white fishnet stockings and high-heeled sandals, they were a work of art unto themselves. What would *they* feel like beneath the palm of my hand, I wondered. And what kind of noise would Lucy make if my fingertips grazed her skin? The same shocked "Hey!" that she'd shrieked when I touched her table? Somehow, from the looks she was giving me in return, I didn't think so.

My producer nudged me and I shook my head, embarrassed, not having heard a word Corrine had said. But Lucy, standing a few feet away, shot me another interested smile, as if she understood exactly what my appraising glances meant.

It all happened quickly after that. Our producer whisked Lucy away to sign some papers and I consulted several other appraisers to get their opinion of the piece's value. My mind instantly and easily refocused on my work. A table in less quality condition had recently sold for a quarter of a million dollars at auction. I could barely contain myself imagining what this item might bring.

When we found ourselves seated in front of the camera, I turned my eyes from the table to Lucy, preparing to launch into the background history of the furniture maker. I am quite adept at my job, my mind filled with little-known facts, but when I looked at

Lucy again, I forgot everything that I'd planned on saying. The make-up crew, in their haste, had removed her garish eye shadow and electrifying lipstick, but had not bothered to replace either. I was staring at a restored canvas, the beauty of her face shining clear now that it was free from the previous hideous coat of shellacking.

"Your beautiful—" I stammered, and then stopped. I'd been about to say, "Your beautiful table," but suddenly that wasn't what I meant at all. Change the 'your' to 'you're,' is what I wanted to tell Lucy. "You're beautiful—" I said again, referring to her this time.

"My table," she said, prompting me when she realized I was tongue-tied. She gave me that same quizzical glance she had earlier, her eyes a softer blue now that they didn't have to compete with the seventies-style shadow. Her cheeks had a natural flush to them, and I wondered what hue they would turn in the throws of passion. If I picked her up and set her down on the table, slid that flimsy dress up her thighs, and bent to kiss in a line down her throat to those loose laces, would her cheeks turn a dark, scarlet blush? Or was she the type whose skin would take on a petal pink glow? I longed to find out, but I could suddenly feel my producer's eyes on me.

"My table" Lucy repeated, waiting.

"Yes," I said, nodding. "Your table is a masterpiece." I put my hand on the top of the surface for reassurance, and the wash of joy swept over me again. I found my words, launching into a history of this fantastic piece of furniture. I told of the maker's background, then described how each table was made by hand, focusing on the length of time it took to create just one leg.

"One of the most interesting aspects of this table," I said, near the end of my spiel, "is that although it appears quite delicate, it is remarkably sturdy."

"Really?" Lucy asked, shooting me a look that sent my mind spinning off into fantasy land all over again. "Sometimes delicate items can fool you."

At that comment, I tried desperately to reboard my train of

thought, but failed. *She* looked delicate, yet I had the feeling that she would last through hours of raucous lovemaking. Was that the hidden message she was trying to tell me? Suddenly, I felt something brush softly against my own leg. It took only a second for me to process that Lucy had slipped out of one high-heeled sandals and was running her stockinged toes up my calf.

I managed to complete my talk, to give her an estimate of the table's worth, but somehow those numbers didn't interest me anymore. The director yelled "cut," and the crew quickly moved across the room to film a segment on wind-up toys. Lucy and I were alone, between the makeshift curtained barriers, still sitting at the table looking at each other.

"You mentioned that it was surprisingly sturdy," Lucy said in a low voice. I watched as she ran her tongue along her top lip, as if she were tasting something sweet. The gesture tugged at me, and I wanted to lean forward and do the same thing to her, run my own tongue along both of her lips before taking her in my arms and kissing her. I took a deep breath, trying to analyze what she had just said.

"Yes," I nodded, "these tables have undergone stress tests. While some pieces are more for show than actual use, your table could easily support five hundred pounds."

"Wow," Lucy said, her mouth, pure and naked of lipstick, curving into a smile. "That's a lot of weight—three or four adults—when all it has to support is two."

This was all the encouragement I needed. Quickly, I motioned to a crew member and asked him to help me put the table into one of our back storage rooms. "I need a little more time to appraise it," I said, using my most business-like tone. The man didn't concern himself with the explanation. Without hesitating, he and I hoisted the table together and brought it to one of the private rooms. Lucy followed, staring at me with what I can only describe as lustfully energetic looks.

Finally alone, I shut the door and lifted Lucy into my arms. I nuzzled into her neck as I carried her over to the table. She smelled delicious, spicy and exotic, and I sat her down on the edge of the table and began to kiss her skin. Lucy sighed, then leaned back fully onto the table, spreading her thighs and raising her arms over her head.

I didn't know where to start first. I wanted to keep kissing her, but I also wanted to peel off her dress and simply look at her body. As when I'm appraising a piece of furniture, I needed to know what I was working with. Lucy took over for me, slipping the dress over her head and then sprawling out in her white satin bra and panties, white fishnets, garter belt, and sandals still on.

The room we were in contained several other pieces of furniture, including a full-length, gilt-edged mirror. I hurried to position it against the wall next to the table, and then grabbed Lucy around the waist and slid her toward me. I kissed her in a line down her body, starting with her lips and then moving to the hollow of her neck, her delicate collarbones, down to her breasts—where I lingered until she arched her back and moaned. Slowly, I kissed my way toward her satin-clad pussy, and when I reached it, I could smell the scent of her arousal.

I licked her through her panties first, just teasing her with my tongue pressed hard against that shiny material. Then I helped her out of the undergarment and began to French kiss her pussy, using my fingers to hold open her lips while my tongue made soft and slow circles around her clit.

After a moment, I looked into the mirror to see Lucy's face. Her head was turned to the side, mouth open and eyes shut. Her hair had come free from the ponytail and it fell loose to her shoulders. Now, brushed flat instead of teased, it perfectly framed her beautiful face. A face which I suddenly recognized—

"Oh, God," I said.

"Yes," Lucy sighed, "Oh, God, it's great."

"No," I stood looking down at her. "I know you."

She opened her eyes and locked onto my gaze. "Yes," she said, "I'm Lucy. We met out there." Her cheeks were flushed with pleasure, a soft pink as I'd imagined they would be, but her face was composed. She looked a lot more at ease than I felt, my cock throbbing beneath my slacks, desperate for contact with the warm, wet mouth of her sex. Still, I had to get something clear.

"You're not some—" I wanted to say 'hick,' but changed my mind quickly, "some innocent who just brought a table to be appraised," I said, watching as she pushed herself into a semi-upright position on the table, leaning up on one elbow. With her free hand, she began to stroke her naked pussy, slowly and sensuously teasing herself while I watched. She seemed to be waiting to see when I'd get it, and finally, when she tilted her head back as the sensations washed over her, I knew precisely who she was. I'd seen the look on her face before, at a recent auction in New York. Upon winning the piece she was after, she leaned her head back and sighed, the same look of ultimate pleasure on her face.

"You're Lucinda Daniels," I said, undoing my slacks now, unable to wait any longer. "You work for Rowen-McLean."

She nodded, her hands helping to guide me between her parted thighs. The contact of my cock with the dreamy wetness of her sex made me momentarily lose track of my thoughts. I plunged inside her and she let out that same, pleasurable sigh again, her hand going up to her throat, fingers beating there as if attempting to still her pounding pulse.

I stopped trying to figure it all out at that point, driving in even deeper inside her. The table supported our weight, but I needed to feel her in my grip. Grabbing her around the waist, I lifted her into my arms and then pulled her down on me. Then, inspired, I took her over to the wall and pressed her against that antique mirror. I couldn't get deep enough inside her, slamming into her willing cunt and then pulling out to the tip, then slamming in again to make her sigh like that. She dragged her fingernails down my back and I had the vision of what they looked like, that obscene emerald green raking against my skin, leaving marks I'd have to remember this by. Suddenly, those nails didn't seem so offensive. There was something sexy in the whole slutty attire—fishnets still in place, sandal-clad feet hooked around my thighs.

"God, Jonathan, I'm going to come," Lucy said softly, and I took her to that fantasy place with me, fucking her harder and faster until she leaned down and bit my shoulder as the climax flew through her. I came a second after, pumping my cock inside her as those wave-like contractions washed over it.

There were several moments when I simply held her in my arms, leaning against the mirror, my eyes closed, breathing deeply. Then I carried her back to the wonderful table and set her down. She looked at me with a coy expression I hadn't seen before.

"It worked, you know," she said softly.

"I don't understand," I told her, watching sadly as she pulled her dress back over her head, that magnificent body disappearing from view.

"You love the creator's work, and I'm sort of partial to yours," she explained. "But I've never been able to catch your attention at the auctions. You always have your eyes on some piece of furniture or another, never seem aware of the piece of ass that wants you."

"So you came here—" I prompted.

"Somehow, I thought that you might find my get-up exciting." When she said it, I realized she was right. I'd seen her often at the auctions, always dressed in some subdued black suit, elegant pearls around her neck, that white-blonde hair pulled back severely, tiny glasses perched on the end of her perfect nose. I never would have guessed she would doll herself up like this, and I couldn't have suspected that I would have liked it.

"You knew what the table was worth, though," I said, telling her the one thing that nagged at my pride. "You wanted to fool me."

She made it all better with her answer.

"I wanted to *fuck* you," she said, leaning forward to whisper it, her mouth against my ear, hot breath against my skin. "You were always so busy appraising everything, you never had eyes for me."

That made me stop thinking about my job and start thinking about what it would be like to make love to Lucy again, maybe on the four-poster bed I had seen in one of the other storage rooms....

"But you have eyes for me now," she continued, spreading her arms wide and taking the stance of a centerfold model. "So..." her voice was rich with humor. "What do you think I'd fetch?" A pause, and another one of those fantastic, cockteasing lip licks, "I mean, if you were to put me up on auction."

Now, I took a step back, looking her over, taking a second before giving her my estimate. "You know how it is with a rare treasure," I said, pulling her toward me once again. "You can never put a label on something priceless."

Blue Denim Pussy
by Mistress A.

"I want you honest opinion," Sasha said, twirling around in front of Colin, letting him see her colt-like legs, haughty ass, slim waist, all contained in a pair of new and tight-fitting dark denim jeans. He didn't respond immediately, taking in the way she looked. Sleek in her long-sleeved black blouse, her birch-colored hair up in a ponytail, gray-green eyes wide while she waited for his answer. Still, he couldn't actually think of anything to say. Nothing except the fact that he was going to fuck her. Here. Now.

"Tell me," she urged, tilting her head to look past him at her own reflection in the dressing room mirror. "I mean, what do you think?"

Still silent, he took one step toward her in the small space and grabbed hold of her hand. His fingers slid upward to close firmly around her delicate wrist, like a pair of handcuffs snapping shut. Something in the gesture made Sasha forget what she was asking and pay attention to the looks Colin was giving her.

"Come here," he said, and she closed the space between them as he placed his free palm over the crotch of her jeans and let her feel his large hand against her cunt. Instantly, she rested her pussy on his hand, pressed into him, and he began to do the most intricate, marvelous things with his fingers. Dancing them up and down. Massaging her pussy through the denim. Stroking just hard enough for her to lean her head back and sigh.

This was obviously the response he was looking for, and Colin quickly sat on the padded bench running the length of the room and he moved Sasha so that she was cradled on his lap. Slowly, but firmly, he continued to rub her cunt through the Levis. He paid attention to every touch, obviously on a mission. She helped, letting him know exactly what she wanted, pushing up with her hips to meet his stroking fingertips as he responded to each move. Focused on bringing her pleasure, he worked harder, firmer, then slid one finger between two buttons in the fly to touch her naked skin.

The feel of his hand on her was electrifying. Just his finger on the space above her pubic hair. Yes, of course, he'd touched her there before. But this was different somehow. Being fingered like this with her clothes still on made Sasha feel the urgency in what they were doing. He pushed down, searching, and his fingertip plunged into the wetness that had already seeped through her nether lips. Withdrawing his hand, he licked his finger clean, then resumed his pussy massage through her jeans.

Closing her eyes, Sasha stifled a moan. Christ, it felt amazing. If he touched her clit with his middle finger, pressed it right up against the seam of her Levis, she could come. Colin guessed this, and he sat her on one hand, and did exactly what she wanted. Tapping against her clit, harder as she got closer to climax, he stroked her cunt until she was almost there. Almost—

"Take them off."

Sasha opened her eyes, stunned, at that point of almost coming that had made her brain slow down in direct correlation to the rate that her heart beat had speeded up.

"Just to your knees. Now."

The urgency had her fumbling. She stood, a wreck, and tried to unbutton the jeans, but found her fingers useless. Colin did the job, pulling hard and popping them open, then sliding the tight jeans down her lean thighs. He went on his knees in front of her, pressing his lips against her white panties, breathing her scent in through that sliver of cotton. Then these were pulled down, too, and he pushed her up against the cold glass of the dressing room mirror and licked at her pussy with his eager, ready tongue.

Sasha gripped onto Colin's shoulder, breathless, as he made those crazy spirals around her clit. She'd been on the brink from the decadent pussy massage, and now Colin was replicating those actions with his tongue. Around and around the tip went. Teasing and tricking, bumping up against her clit and then leaving it alone to throb desperately, urgently. He kissed her inner thighs for a moment, to give her a chance to miss him. Then, back at the game, he nudged her clit, pushing, before finally ringing her pulsing gem with his lips and sucking. Just sucking.

Oh, yeah, Sasha thought, too tongue-tied to say the words out loud. *Oh, yeah.* Captured by the jeans and held upright by Colin's hands around her waist, she let her body relax into the climax. Sliding into it. Drifting into it. Helpless to stop herself. But then, she didn't want to stop. Did she?

When she opened her eyes, Colin was still helping—helping her take off her jeans and folding them into a neat square. "We'll get these," he said. "Because if you didn't guess from my response, I like them."

Then he was turning her, hands flat against the mirror, his body behind her, letting her feel the promise of his cock pressed against her ass. Letting her know with a single look at her eyes in the mirror exactly what was going to happen next—

Curtain Call
by Thomas S. Roche

We should get one thing straight from the outset: Drew wasn't in the habit of taking her clothes off in front of strangers. Sure, she might have thought about it once or twice, but she never figured she'd actually do it. *Especially* not strangers who knew where she lived.

She'd been a little uncomfortable when she'd first taken the apartment; it was weird for her, a country girl, to be living in the City with a picture window right across the alley from another apartment. The rental agent had explained that this apartment building had been built before the other one—that once the picture window had looked out over a beautiful view of the lake. But a few years ago, the high-rise had gone up across the alley, and now the view was of some other person's living room. Not that it had inspired the landlord to lower the rent or anything—but Drew didn't care; she was just glad to have an apartment after her long and frustrating search.

Besides, the second she'd seen the picture window facing the apartment across the alley, her mind had turned to the idea of taking her clothes off in front of it, and the deal was closed. Not that she thought she'd actually do it, mind you. Drew wasn't exactly a good girl; in fact she really wasn't a good girl; in fact, she wasn't anything even remotely like a good girl, but she drew the line at taking her clothes off in public. Her provocative clothing was nothing more than a matter of physical geography, albeit one she relished. She didn't go out of her way to display her full hips, her large breasts, her thick, strong legs—they just sort of displayed themselves, and she liked it that way. Drew's tasteful office attire was always a little dressier than was necessary, maybe even slightly tighter than was necessary, showing off the swell of her tits and the curves of her ass. It never crossed the line of propriety, mind you, not quite "slutty," just, how would you say it, "body-comfortable"—that worked. She drew more approving looks than she would have thought possible when she was the quote-unquote "overweight" ugly duckling living in Wisketaw, Minnesota. Funny how that happened.

Guys at the office were always asking her for dates, but after all, Drew had moved here to "find" herself, that obscure thing people were supposed to do when they turned twenty-five or maybe twenty-nine, or in Drew's case twenty-seven, two years late or early, depending on your perspective.

So Drew turned her admirers down for their dinners and movies and impossible-to-get seats at Miss Saigon—and stayed home, reveling in the pleasures of her new apartment. And the pleasures of that big picture window.

Drew would stay home weekend nights, often having turned down a date or two from the technicians up on the fifth floor or the lawyers on seven—most of the bastards married—once, even, the Fed-Ex dude, who she'd been sure was gay. She just couldn't stand the thought of going through another love affair when she finally had an apartment to herself, a place where she could stretch out on the expansive, luxurious floor—more luxurious than a couch would have been, even had she been able to afford one—and ease out of her office clothes, enjoying the sight of herself in the big mirror on the closet door, enjoying the sight of her sexy garter belt, stockings, tight panties, sometimes even no panties, the knowledge of that making her uncomfortably but deliciously wet all day long. She could put a porn movie in the VCR, one of those "women's erotica" movies she'd discovered at the big-city "feminist porn shop" recently. The porn was disgustingly PC compared to the sleaze her ex-boyfriends used to want to watch with her, but somehow unbelievably sexy precisely because it was aimed at her, like it represented the fact that everyone in the world knew she was masturbating right now—or something. She would put on the movies and stretch out on the floor with a bottle of red wine and her vibrator and maybe even a dildo or two, enjoying the feeling of being horribly, terribly, irrevocably bad—not because she was watching porn or masturbating with sex toys, but because she was drinking red wine on that immaculate white carpet, and her anxiety about losing part of her cleaning deposit was matched only by the decadent thrill she felt in thinking about dumping the whole bottle over her naked body and laughing about it—because she was going to be alone in this apartment for a long, delicious time.

Drew would keep the curtains closed on that window, thinking about whoever was beyond it, thinking about what they were doing. Maybe whoever lived there had their curtains open and were doing nasty things in front of the window, wishing Drew would open her curtains so she could see them. The thought gave her a thrill. Drew was as much a closet voyeur as a closet exhibitionist. Once when she lived in Minnesota she'd heard her downstairs neighbors fucking—she'd fantasized about that for months, still fantasized about it sometimes when she was masturbating. When she'd found out, weeks later, that *two women* lived there, a handsome diesel dyke and a curvy femme, that only fueled Drew's savoring of her illicit carnal knowledge. There's something so delicious about things you're not supposed to know, like what two lesbians sound like in the throes of lovemaking.

Now, she would fantasize about the people on the other side of those curtains. She would think about them watching her as she looked at porn and stroked herself, as she spread her broad thighs, as she tugged her skimpy panties to one side and slipped the silicon dildo smoothly into her body, as she turned the vibrator on high and pressed it to her clit, as she came, screaming, to the images on the TV screen and the knowledge of sexual beings right behind her curtains, wanting to watch her and being denied. More than once Drew left her window open behind those closed curtains, watching the red fabric ripple in the 25th-floor breeze, knowing that wind might carry her orgasmic screams to the people across the alley, or—and this never failed to get her off —the people *in* the alley many floors below.

But Drew never actually *opened* the curtains—not even when she was just hanging out, to see who lived there. That might have spoiled the fantasy, she figured. Or would it?

Drew discovered her very favorite video one night when she was just a little tipsy from a glass of wine and pleasantly satisfied by take-out Chateaubriand from Francesca's Italian Restaurant— she'd just gotten a mid-month paycheck and wanted to treat herself. There wasn't a bit of irony in it, because Drew watched a lot of videos, having grown up in a place where "women's erotica" meant *Cosmopolitan* articles on "How to Give Your Man Orgasms!" At this point, she'd seen practically every so-called "sex-positive" video, both lesbian and straight, that the sex shop rented, and she was starting in on the commercial stuff out of sheer desperation. But somehow she'd missed "The Hungry Gaze" in her first whirlwind tour through the video section. It had been made by a tiny lesbian erotica company in Minneapolis. It was an interesting coincidence, to be sure, and one that would drive Drew to even more perverse fantasies of sexual exhibition. But given how many videos Drew had watched since moving to the City, there really wasn't that much irony in it.

That is to say, in the fact that "The Hungry Gaze" was a thirty-minute short about a woman who showed off for her neighbor in front of the picture window of her high-rise apartment building.

Drew came three times, the remains of the Chateaubriand forgotten, the red wine serving only to hydrate her in gulps between her frenzied bursts of self-fucking and desperately rewinding the tape, muttering "Come on, come on" while she stroked her wet pussy and listened to the annoying whine of the rewinding VCR. Then she started all over again.

It didn't bother her one bit that the woman on the tape was showing off for another woman, despite the fact that Drew thought of herself as exclusively straight. Hell, the woman across the alley in the video was more handsome than any of Drew's boyfriends, and the woman showing off was a woman more like Drew than like the blow-dried prom queens she saw in commercial porn and even a lot of the more artistic stuff. Her yummy broad ass and rounded hips were cinched lusciously into a corset, her luscious tits spilling out with their bright rings dancing for the camera as the woman ground her hips and spread her legs, exposing her shaved pussy as she slipped her fingers inside. Across the alley, the other woman, a skinny dyke with a DA, lay naked except for a stained jock strap, fondling her small tits and pulling the cotton garment away so she could rub her pussy as she watched. The tension between the two women, even across the illusory gap between buildings, was palpable and drove Drew into a new fury.

"Fuck," muttered Drew hungrily as she pumped her pussy yet again. "Sign me up."

But what really turned her on was the fact that the woman was showing off— and doing it in front of a window. It made Drew think about who might be watching her if she just *happened* to leave the drapes open one night....

And that's when Drew did it. Maybe the fact that she gulped the remainder of the wine before she opened the curtains is what gave her the guts to do it.

Or maybe she really was a slut after all.

She kept her garter belt on, but took off the bra, before she opened the curtains. She loved the way the garter belt framed her broad thighs, her wide hips, her hourglass figure, drawing attention to the wispy blonde hair on her pussy.

She wanted to peek first, but Drew told herself she shouldn't. There was such an intense, hard thrill to just opening the curtains— and if there was someone standing there watching her, she could always pull the curtains closed like it was an honest mistake.

But there wasn't. The curtains across the alley were open, but the apartment was dark. Whoever lived there had gone to bed.

But rather than closing the curtains and going to bed herself, as she knew she should have done, Drew dragged her one kitchen chair over to the middle of the room and, dragging the towel with her pussy-and-lube moistened vibrator and dildo on it over with her, she sat down on the chair.

Was there someone there in the dark watching her?

"You could get arrested for this," she told herself out loud, and spread her legs.

She could feel the erotic tension flowing from her fingertips to her full breasts, her swollen nipples, her spread thighs. She could hear herself moan uncontrollably as she rubbed her wet pussy and her engorged clit. Someone was watching her. Man or woman, she didn't care. One of the lawyers from work, finally realizing what a slutty whore this third-floor secretary was. One of the dykes from the video, treated unexpectedly to a hot show while she fucked herself on her couch. One of her ex-boyfriends, suddenly realizing what a hot piece he'd lost hold of. It didn't matter. Whoever he was, he was slipping his hand into his briefs, roused from his slumber to appreciate Drew's wanton display. Whoever she was, she was slipping out of her panties, stroking her pussy, made instantly wet and dripping by the sight of Drew showing herself off. Whoever he was, he was taking his cock, now hard, out of his Jockeys and stroking it, his hand gripping tightly as he pumped his hard flesh, as his eyes roved over Drew's mostly-naked body. Whoever she was, she was spreading her legs wide and fucking herself the same way Drew was fucking her own pussy, a six-inch dildo, the really thick one, working its way in and out of her as the vibrator hummed on her clit. She was going to come. She was going to come.

Whoever she was, she was transfixed by the pumping motions of Drew's hips. Whoever he was, he couldn't take his eyes off the dancing fullness of Drew's breasts. Whoever they were, they looked into Drew's bright blue eyes and wanted her, wanted her bad— wanted her in a way no boyfriend or casual sexual interest had ever wanted her, because they'd never realized what a fucking slut she was, and how much she loved it. They wanted her, because Drew was as much of an exhibitionist as they wanted her to be.

God, she was coming—coming again! Drew felt the orgasm bursting through her pussy as lifted herself up and down on the chair so she could push the thick dildo harder into her, rubbing her cervix, slapping her G-spot mercilessly as the vibrator drove her over the edge. She was coming, and moaning at the top of her lungs, not caring that the window was open or even, as she finished coming, that the light had gone on across the alley.

Not even caring that the hottest guy she'd ever seen was standing there with his dick in his hand, his eyes wide, watching her. Not even caring that he came as she came, and that he couldn't take his eyes off her, even as she finished coming and ground to a halt on the tiny kitchen chair, watching him, transfixed by the sight of his hard cock spurting come onto the carpet.

He didn't look embarrassed—this bastard was shameless! He'd turned the light on so Drew could see him, so she could see how much she was turning him on.

"Oh fuck, oh fuck, oh fuck!!" said Drew to herself as she watched the guy blowing her kisses and then running for something out of sight of the window.

Drew jumped up, still mostly naked, her face flushing hot as she went to close the curtains. But the guy got back before her, and he held up the piece of paper.

Drew couldn't help herself. She started laughing. Her face flushed an even deeper red.

It was his phone number.

She stood there looking at him and laughing for what must have been a full minute. When she was finished laughing she just smiled, looking foolishly across the alley as he held eye contact and kept nodding and pointing at the number.

Drew heard herself give a surprisingly girlish giggle.

Drew mouthed, "Thank you," laughing again, blushing hot. She blew him a kiss, pulled the curtains closed, and went to bed.

Dirty Pictures
by Beau Morgan

Jesse won't meet my eyes.

"Pretty girl," I say softly, "look at me." She doesn't, but I come in close with the camera, anyway, wanting to capture that vulnerable expression, the shyness that surrounds her. Her full lower lip is plumped out, pouting. She tosses her long hair so that it falls into her face instead of away from it. Wisps of soft gold streak over her cheeks and mouth.

"Don't be ashamed," I tell her. "This is art. There's nothing to feel bad about."

She won't lift her face, despite my patience, my soothing tone. Instead, she actually does the opposite of what I want, burying her face into the pillows in the center of the bed. The brass bed is in the middle of the room. It's not mine, a piece of furniture borrowed for the shoot. But the bed works with the lines of her body, with the shape of her face. There's something old-fashioned about Jesse, an aura from another time. As a backdrop, the brass bed compliments her.

I put down the camera, walk over to her, slide my hands through her blonde hair and pull it off her face. I tilt her head back forcefully, and she gives me a frightened little half-smile, as if she thinks I might kiss her, as if she might like that.

Stepping away again, I frame her with my lens, catch her naked breasts, her flat belly, the rise of her slender hips. The sheet covers the lower portion of her body, and she hasn't allowed me to pull it off her. Each time I artfully arrange the cotton sheet to reveal more of her naked from, she moves, slips back underneath, begs me to give her just a little more time.

"Look at me," I say again, and now she doesn't lower her chin, but she closes her eyes. I take the picture anyway. Her long lashes stand out against her pale skin. Her chin is at an angle I would consider defiant if I didn't know how scared she is.

Sometimes when you shoot real people, not models, they freeze. Jesse is not a professional model. She's a nineteen-year-old kid, young looking for her age, but with the perfect appearance for S., my patron. I try to help her relax by flattering her, by encouraging her to talk about herself.

"You never thought you'd be a pin-up, did you?"

She doesn't answer.

"You know you're beautiful," I try next. Despite my best efforts, Jesse won't relax. It's time to choose a different method.

"Lie down," I say, still using my most patient voice. I stand beside the bed and take the sheet all the way off. Jesse tries to cover her nakedness with her hands, crossing them over her bare pussy, shielding herself from me. She leaves her breasts uncovered, and I take the picture like that, on the bed looking down at her. One shot. Then she turns her face to the left, tucks her chin against her shoulder. Her cheeks are flaming. I can't remember ever being that shy. I feel ancient compared to her, even though I'm only six years her senior.

"Move your hands," I command, bending on my knees and coming to rest between her legs. I want a picture taken up her body, up the line of it, catching her shaved mons, her concave belly, the curve of her breasts. The curlicues of brass that make up the headboard are behind her, the pattern of metal a tangle in soft focus. I visualize her hands gripped into the railing, my body pressed hot and hard against hers. The image is only in my head. I've got work to do.

She fans her delicate fingers apart, but doesn't take her hands away. I shoot the picture, then cradle my camera in one hand and reach to grab hold of her fingers, to move them, to arrange her as I want.

"Please," she says softly, "another second."

Squeezing her fingertips, I set her hand on her hip, release it, and take the shot like that, one palm over her cunt, her other hand away, a half-revealed picture of her pussy. At the camera's click, she moves her free hand back, hiding again.

I stand and go to my wardrobe, riffling around for a sheer silk scarf. As I drape it over Jesse's naked body, I imagine the photographs I would like to take of her: Jesse bound, her hands over her head, a rope—not handcuffs—capturing her wrists to the bed frame. I picture her blindfolded, frightened, tears running down her cheeks while the flash catches her off-guard, the white light reaching her even through the blindfold.

The scarf seems to help her. Even though it doesn't hide anything, it's a layer of protection between her body and the camera. She breathes deeply and then sighs. I take hold of her wrists and bring them over her head.

"Stay," I tell her, the way you'd speak to a dog. The pose elongates her body. Jesse trembles, but keeps in place for me. Perhaps, all I needed to do was talk rough to her, talk straight. She locks her wrists together, one over the other, as if they actually are bound together. Maybe we're both visualizing the same things.

I take the picture, then have her roll onto her stomach, and I crouch over her to take a close-up shot between her spread thighs. Her ass tightens, and I tell her to relax, then move around her, staring at her, finding each shot and taking it.

S. adores girls like this one. The shy young flowers. The nubile princesses. I have Jesse get on all fours, next, staring at me, directly at me. I remove the scarf, pause to admire her stark naked form. This is the hardest for her, the most difficult, meeting my gaze while I invade her with the lens. She shuts her eyes. I won't have it.

"Look at me."

"Please..." she says.

"Now."

Something in my voice makes her obey. She opens her eyes wide and I take the picture. When I develop the black and white prints, her blue eyes will turn a clear gray. I focus on them, reading the fear in them, fear mixed with longing.

For the last shot, I move behind her. She can't see me. I get close to her body, close enough to smell the sweet scent of her sex. I use my hands to stretch her legs even wider. I take a picture lying on my back, beneath her, looking up. A tight shot of her pussy. The hungry mouth between her legs open and ready, willing. The muscles in her arms start to tremble. I visualize fucking her with my camera, spreading her lips wide apart around the lens, sliding the black tube inside her.

Taking the picture.

Erotic Explorations
by Gabriella Wise

I just came. My fingertips still smell of my fragrant juices and my legs are trembling and weak. It's always the same for me right after I climax. I feel washed out, limp as a rag, but relaxed, as if I've just received a long, hot oil massage. In fact, when I *have* treated myself to a real massage, I never feel quite as refreshed afterwards as I do following a mind-shattering, body-shaking orgasm.

Usually, I have my best climaxes while astride my husband's cock. I know just how to do it. I climb on top of Alex's firm body with my slender thighs spread apart, and I pump, sliding my wet pussy up and down his straining hard-on. He reaches out and touches my firm breasts, pinches my nipples, makes me arch my back as I work him. I like being on top, riding him, like being able to watch the expressions change on his handsome face. His dark brown eyes stare into mine, and his lips pull back in a sort of grimace, as if the pleasure is so strong that it's almost painful.

But just now, I used my favorite vibrator, climaxing with that instead. Or, rather, climaxing with that *first*. My special toy is a small, battery-powered job only slightly bigger than a tube of lipstick. However, the size is deceptive. Although small, the toy is one powerful fucking machine. You can hear the engine throbbing away clear down the hall, which is why I masturbate only when I'm alone. At least, I did before tonight.

I've been married for nearly three years. We have a vibrant sex life, my husband and I. We work hard to make each other's fantasies come true. When Alex confessed a desire for doing it in public, I treated him to a wild time in the back row of The Mann's Chinese movie theater in Hollywood, making absolutely sure that we saw none of the movie. And when Alex learned my weakness for fucking under the spray of a hot shower, he surprised me one morning, climbing in behind me and making me late for work in the most pleasurable way possible.

But Alexander's job takes him out of town often, and this is why I bought myself the sex toy. Not as a cock replacement, you understand, but as a way to pass the time while he's gone. I didn't tell him I'd bought it, never used it with him, or when he was in town. Never, until tonight.

Alex was due back from his latest trip tomorrow. We'd had steamy phone sex each night he was away, and I had every intention of picking him up at the airport tomorrow evening, dressed only in a long black trench coat, stockings with garters, and my favorite spike heels. I'd choreographed the scene in my head, visualizing us fucking against our convertible in a deserted corner of the parking lot. I could see each step in my mind: Alex lifting my coat in back, slipping his cock between my thighs, taking me hard and fast. Maybe I'd planned it too well, because simply the thought of what I was going to do had me all excited. So excited that I decided to take care of my urge with my special toy, sliding the vibrator deep inside of my cunt and letting the mechanical vibrations throb through me.

This is exactly how Alex found me.

He'd changed his plans as a surprise, cutting his trip short and arriving a day ahead of schedule. Rather than call from the airport, he took a taxi home, only to discover me in the center of our bed, my long red hair fanned out on the pillow like a gingery halo, my legs spread wide apart as I worked the vibrator back and forth between them. Yes, I should have heard him unlock the front door and call out my name, but I didn't. This is because I was wearing a headset and listening on my Walkman to a woman's voice describing a particularly dirty act. What a treat. I'd never listened to a sex tape before, but I'd bought one on a whim, and now, my vibrator charged up, my body ready, I'd given in.

And it had turned me on.

When Alex walked into the bedroom, suit jacket over one arm, tie askew, I'm sure he thought he'd sneak up on me in bed, fast asleep, curled up with one arm hugging a pillow. Instead, he was greeted with the vision of me in the throws of passion, ferociously fucking myself with a vibrating wand while listening to the husky voice of a nameless, faceless storyteller as she purred her way through an X-rated fantasy. And when he found me like this, all he did was watch. Silently, hungrily, standing in our doorway and staring in awe. Staring with such intensity, that suddenly, I opened my eyes, sensing his presence. For some reason, I wasn't frightened or embarrassed at all, just startled and about one millisecond away from coming.

"Don't stop," he said, loud enough now for me to hear him over the tape. "Keep going, Angel. Keep going for me."

I couldn't have stopped if he'd paid me. The urgency of the impending climax was simply too much to deny. My body started shaking with the powerful vibrations and I came, staring into my husband's deep brown eyes, listening to the woman on the tape talk about how a big, fucking cock was going in and out of her. Plunging into her dripping snatch until she could feel it at the back of her throat.

I've always had a thing for dirty talk. Hearing these words while on display for Alex made me climax more fiercely than I ever had. But when I was finished, I did start to feel slightly odd. I'd never thought about sharing this part of my sex life with Alex, never had tried to imagine how he would feel about it. Flicking off the vibrator and shrugging off the headphones, I waited to see what Alex would have to say about his discovery. He didn't say anything. Not a word. He simply undressed in a hurry and came forward, still staring at me as if I were some fantasy creature who had appeared in his real-life bed. The look on his face made me aroused all over again. This time, I was ready for his cock. And, oh man, it was ready for me.

"You're so fucking sexy," Alex said, reaching the bed, as if pulled toward me by the strength of his rod. "I've never seen you look like that." He paused, searching for the right word. "Untamed." He said it as if he were in a way naming me, and then he climbed on the bed and took hold of both my wrists in one of his hands.

"But, Angel," he said, positioning himself over my body, "I know something you don't."

I looked up at him, waiting, sensing that his cock was just a sliver of space away from my slick pussy lips and desperate for his skin to meet mine. "What do you know?" I asked, when it became apparent he wouldn't continue until I spoke.

"I know how to tame you." Then he was moving forward, his body against mine, opening me up with his throbbing rod and sliding inside of me. Automatically, my pussy welcomed him by squeezing, and he sighed and then grinned at me. As if saying that he understood I was testing him, and that he knew he'd be able to pass. Did he ever. He took me for a wild ride. Long and hard, as I'd imagined he would outdoors at the airport. It was his way of saying he'd missed me on his trip, that he'd been desperate to fuck me each night he was gone. His eyes closed and he leaned back, so that I could see the long line of his neck, the taut muscles clenched in his jaw. He was almost there, I sensed it. But I sensed wrong.

Pulling out, Alex moved away from me on our king-sized bed.

"I want to see you do that again."

"What—?" I panted, not understanding.

"Touch yourself for me. This time, with your fingers, while I watch."

I got it now, but I had something of my own to add. "You, too," I whispered, my voice sounding a lot like the woman's on the tape, a cat's purr. At my request, Alex nodded, as if that part of the bargain was understood. He would stroke his cock while I tickled my clit.

Slowly, I brought my hand to my cunt and parted my nether lips. While he watched, I fingered myself, gently because I'd already come once, and softly, because I wanted to make it last. I could feel Alex watching me, his gaze moving from my face to my body, his eyes lingering. It was as if he couldn't decide which part turned him on the most. Watching my expressions change as the arousal worked through me, or staring as I played with myself. Taking it all in, he started to move his hand on his rod, slicked up from my pussy juices.

That turned me on more than I'd have thought. We'd never even come close to doing this before. Sure, I knew that he must occasionally masturbate. I mean, I do, so why wouldn't he? I didn't have a problem with the concept of him jerking off while he was on the road, but it wasn't something we'd discussed, or something we'd ever shared. Now, I wondered why we'd waited this long. It was amazing to see his hand moving up and down on his cock, faster and harder than I'd ever have had the nerve to touch him. When I give him hand jobs, I am careful not to stroke too hard, to hold him too tightly. Now, I had to get closer, to really see his method. He seemed to squeeze the tip when he reached it, then loosen his fist for the ride down, pumping up again and then sliding down. The sound was arousing, as well, a clapping noise as his hand met the skin of his lower belly. I was so mesmerized that, for a moment, I forgot to touch myself. Forgot, until Alex said, "Angel—"

And then I remembered. My fingers picked up their circles, round and round, just barely brushing my clit, and then faster and tighter until I had gotten to the point where I could take a firmer touch. While Alex stared hungrily I used four fingers to give my clit little love taps. This move pushed my husband over the edge.

"Christ, Angel. Spank it," he urged, his hand a blur of motion against his throbbing tool. I followed his command, slapping my fingers harder against my clit, and coming from a combination of this and from the way Alex watched. This climax was nothing like the first. The power radiated throughout my body, from fingertips to toes, shuddering through me and leaving me breathless. And, although we came separately, each bringing ourselves to climax, I felt that we came together. I sensed that Alex felt the same way because he moved to hold me in his sticky embrace, limbs pressed against each other, bodies still trembling.

"I never knew—" Alex started, turning my head so that he could stare down into my eyes. I nodded, because I understood. Never knew that it would turn me on so much to watch him turn himself on. And vice versa. But now we know—how to do it, and how to watch, and I can't wait to turn him on again.

Focus of Attention
by Shane Fowler

The woman's body was wrapped in shiny black vinyl, and her dark hair was piled high up on her head. I sat one table away, watching her. Staring. She wore a zippered dress, tight collar, and knee-high boots. You could have stood her under a shower and the water would have rolled off her clothes. I liked that mental picture, the spray from the shower beading up and streaking, like teardrops, down her water-repellant, bondage-inspired outfit.

Daniel didn't mind that my attention had wavered from him. He poured us each another glass of champagne and then clinked our glasses together, saying softly, "Cheers, baby." I didn't respond.

The object of my desire had midnight-black hair and bright green eyes. Her full lips were slicked with a deep berry red stain. Instantly, I imagined that lipstick smeared along the flat of my belly, and lower, decorating my shaved pussy with ruby streaks. I pictured her crouched between my thighs, the glossy juices of my pleasure adding shimmer to her lips, her sea green eyes warm and liquid, radiant with want and need.

"Cat got your tongue?" my husband asked. He reached out and stroked the back of my hand with his fingers. "You'd like that, wouldn't you? You'd like it if that particular pretty pussycat had hold of your tongue... right between her legs."

Maybe this wasn't appropriate chitchat for dinner at a fancy French restaurant. But I was pretty sure that the other diners wouldn't care in the slightest. First off, few spoke English. But more importantly, this wasn't your average restaurant.

Daniel and I were ensconced in a corner table at a decadent nightspot in the fifth district of Paris. A club privé, or *private* club. You need to look like you belong in order to be granted access. The hostesses wear tiny dresses that show everything when they bend over: inner thighs, naked ass, hair or bare. The dimly lit rooms are decorated in black, and the ceiling, stretched over with a glistening plasticine material, rolls like water. Cut-glass mirrors in the dining room reflect the patrons, letting you get a good look at those around you while you eat, but before you *dine*. The mirrors throw a multitude of rainbow lights dancing around the room, and the effect is like being inside a kaleidoscope, twinkling, glimmering, surreal.

But I know the place. I didn't need to observe the exotic decor, the gorgeous waiter-girls. I only had eyes for her.

She winked at me. Her long, mascara-drenched lashes fluttered, and I suddenly knew what she would look like when she came, knew that those ocean eyes would glow even brighter. I could picture her on the bed in the center of the other room, me on top, her crimson, spade-shaped fingernails creating designs down the skin of my naked back.

One of the oddities at this particular club is the double-bed in the center of the second room, a room that serves as both bar and dance arena. Rich velvet curtains from the canopy above the bed shield a mattress sheathed in black satin. In my fantasy, I was the star, grabbing the zipper nestled between this lovely woman's breasts and undoing her dress with my teeth, peeling off that layer of vinyl to reveal her tender skin. I visualized her body as pale all over, no tan lines, no piercings, no tattoos. She didn't need additional adornments. She made the ultimate fashion statement with the collar encircling her slender throat.

Daniel clinked our glasses a second time and I turned toward him. "Are you hungry, Katrina?" he asked me. "Or are you thirsty...?"

My husband has always wanted to see me eat another woman's pussy. In fact, it's his number one fantasy. When we fuck, he describes what I will look like, the way my face will be coated with her sticky sweet juices. The way I'll know exactly how to make her come, spreading the lips of her pussy, using my tongue and my teeth to find her clit, to tug on it gently, to nip it and give it sloppy, wet kisses.

"Thirsty," I answered, knowing what he meant, what he wanted me to say. I lifted my champagne and took a sip. The wetness on my lips was her wetness, the taste her subtle blend.

Daniel sat back again and said, "So look at your little friend again. I know you want to. Stare at her, make goo-goo eyes at her, tell her silently how much you want to eat her, how much you want to press your face into her sopping cunt and make dessert from the creamy nectar of her sex." He smiled at me, his face coldly handsome, his eyes on fire. "You'll know just what to do when you get there, Kat. Stop worrying so much."

As I looked back at the woman, I realized that Daniel was right, I would know what to do to her, how to do it. And I wanted to start doing those things immediately.

At the Deux a Deux, it's couples only. The woman's mate, an older Frenchman with thick silver hair and a James Bond build, watched me lose myself in his wife's beauty. After our dinner plates had been cleared away, he leaned toward me, pointed to himself, and said, "Jean-Pierre." I held my breath as she followed his lead, touching the valley between her breasts with one cardinal red nail and saying, "Claudia."

Jean-Pierre grinned as my gaze flickered between them, from her to him, then back again. He nodded, approvingly, at my own special outfit. I wasn't dressed in the S/M bondage queen gear that Claudia had on, although my trousseau does contain plenty of vinyl. This evening, my husband had chosen a more romantic look for me. Before leaving the hotel, Daniel had brushed my long, chestnut curls, running the boar's bristle brush through my crowning glory until my tresses gleamed. The silky loops fell loose down my back, free-falling over the straps of my floral sundress. Besides the short dress, I wore white stockings, high-heels, and a pair of virginal white panties.

Most girls go pantyless at the club, into the concept of easy access, but Daniel likes to pull my panties down my thighs before we make love, revealing me slowly. I *know* that most girls go without undergarments, because this was our second trip to the Deux a Deux. The first time we visited the club was a year ago.

We'd been discussing it for months ahead of time, ever since Daniel had spotted a reference on a kinky Web site. My interest was piqued by the idea of a civilized club created solely for introducing couples to couples, a place that allowed people to strip down and fuck while others watched.

From the moment the hostess looked us over through her peep hole and opened the door, we were comfortable at the Deux a Deux. The surroundings are subtle; the patrons unusually good looking. On our first visit, we ate a sumptuous meal, made our way into the second room to drink and size people up, and then waited to see what would happen. We wanted to understand how the place worked, what the rules were, the social clues.

In the bar/dance area, we settled ourselves on a deep red sofa and made casual eye contact with the couples nearby. We drank glasses of champagne, watched a few brave dancers grooving on the slick floor, and continued to wait. After listening to several songs, we noticed a trail of couples slowly making their way down a winding staircase to... we didn't know what. Finally, we followed, walking across the dance floor to the stairway. I felt the eyes of other patrons watch me as I reached out for the cool metal railing to follow as a guide to the room down below.

On the second floor, things were much simpler. There was no more of the blasé flirtatiousness of the room above. Women were seated on the floor, nursing from their lovers' cocks. Men had bent their ladies over at the waist and were taking them from behind. It was a debauched underground etching from the 1890s come to life. And for us, it was fantasy turned to reality.

I think my husband would have come in his pants if I hadn't pulled them down his thighs and gotten in front of him, mouth open, tongue out to stroke the straining shaft of his powerful rod. As I sucked him, Daniel staked out the room, and once he'd come for the first time of the evening, he moved us into position next to a beautiful threesome. The group consisted of two women and one man, and I watched, entranced, as the blonde vixen dined on the brunette's pussy. The fourth member of the party, the husband of one of the girls, stood a few feet back, also viewing the grope-fest, his own hand wrapped around his meat, pulling and tugging. I understood why he was content with being an observer. The X-rated scenario was extreme. Their moans and sighs, slurping sounds. The way the women treated each other, at first touching tentatively and gently, but giving way to heated strokes as the intensity built.

On our left, a beautiful woman in tight leather slacks knelt on the floor, pleasing her man with the skilled affections of a ravenous mouth. Her lover's attention was captivated by another couple, next to him, and his hands were full with the breasts of a woman not his own.

Daniel and I were among the youngest of the crowd, but we were not the most outgoing. Couples in their fifties and sixties got comfortable on the leather couches and pleasured each other. At first, being a part of the action was too frightening for me. I wanted to watch, but not take part. I wanted to *be* watched, but not be taken by anyone but Daniel. He shielded me in the beginning, using his body as a buffer zone. He bent me over a plush, padded seat and fucked me doggy-style, and when he began to find his beat, his hand only naturally connected with the naked skin of my ass....

All heads turned at the noise. All eyes looked up.

"That got their attention," Daniel said. I blushed so hard that my cheeks seemed illuminated in the dim light. Spanking must be a no-no at the Deux a Deux, or if not a faux pas, then a very rare event. But rather than turn away, the patrons moved in closer. Daniel, always in charge, spanked me again. Harder. Louder. I gripped onto the seat and steeled myself for the ride. He pumped me, bucking his hips into mine, grabbing my long hair and wrapping it around one fist. He used my curls to keep me steady, pulling my head up so that I was forced to see the people watching, insisting that I open my eyes when he realized I had squeezed them shut.

"They're watching you, Kat," Daniel hissed.

I didn't answer.

"Open your eyes, baby. You're the show tonight. You're on center stage."

People moved in closer, tight around us. Hands reached out to touch me, to stroke the skin that he was spanking. And despite my shyness, despite my earlier reservations, I found myself enthralled by the feeling of so many fingertips on me, so many probing hands.

Daniel grabbed my hips and fucked harder into me, my cunt making a sweet slurping sound each time he connected. There were women at my level now, on their knees next to me, peering at my face, kissing my cheeks, watching my reaction each time Daniel's strong hand connected with my quickly reddening ass. There were men close by, pinching my nipples until my skin seemed to scream, digging their fingers into my heated flesh.

"Kiss her back," Daniel said, indicating the woman closest to me, a knock-out redhead whose lips were mere millimeters from my own. I bit my bottom lip instead, dying to kiss her, but scared again. I looked into her eyes, then turned my head to look over my shoulder at Daniel as I came.

He said, "Kat... okay, Kat," leaned his head back and followed me, diving deep into bliss.

We left right after, confused and excited. Fueled with enough fodder for a year's worth of fantasies. I remember that the women were lovely, but I can picture no faces, only the heat of the bodies and the warmth of their touch.

But that was last time.

On our return trip, things were different. We were more experienced and I was less bashful. And then there was Claudia. I simply could not turn away from her. She had that entrancing look of a lusty vampire. With me in my pristine outfit, and her in bad-girl black, we made an interesting couple. Now, really, Daniel and I make an interesting couple. He's 6'3", with auburn hair cut short, a goatee that frames his fierce smile, and gray eyes that only come alive after dark. Wolf's eyes. He has a way of looking at me that lets me know what he's thinking. Usually, he's thinking about sex, so my life as a mind reader is pretty simple. I'm 28 and I have a petite build — 5'3", 105 pounds. Daniel can lift me over his head as if bench pressing me.

But Claudia and I, well, we would *scream* as a twosome. We'd fit together with ease, my face between her legs, her thighs wrapped around my body, limbs entwined, hair spread about us like the glossy coats rich women wear.

Even so, I had the problem of communicating this to her. At the Deux a Deux, the majority of the patrons are French. It's not a place that many Americans know about. On the nights Daniel and I have visited, we have been the only native English-speakers. So everything I wanted to tell Claudia, I needed to do with gestures, with kisses, with my hands on her pale skin. Before dessert was served, she and her husband had slid closer to us. She put her hand on my thigh, beneath the tablecloth. He leaned toward us and watched as she turned my chin toward hers and kissed me.

All fear fell away. I embraced her slender body and held her to me. I kissed her deeply, then let my mouth move from her lips to that beckoning charm dangling from her collar. I bit this and tugged, my teeth gripping into the cold metal loop, pulling her upward by that slim circle of silver. She moaned loudly and I could feel myself smile. Then she took one of my hands and placed it on her lap, and I let my fingers wander down to the hem of her dress and between her legs, discovering not only that she had no panties on, but that she was shaved bare, like me. I let my fingers move down further, stroking her knee-high vinyl boots, slipping my fingertips along that sleek material and then back up to her sweet, supple skin again.

When it looked like I might unzip Claudia's dress and take her right on the table, the hostesses swarmed around us, urging us in French and broken English to move into the second room.

"Come—"

"This way—"

"Si vous plait—"

It was obvious they didn't want us to fuck in the dining room. My hand tight in Claudia's, we followed, but rather than seat ourselves on the banks of cloth-covered sofas, we moved directly to the bed.

Other diners had already settled in this room, but no one had yet dared climb onto the mattress between the canopy. Claudia pressed me forward, onto the bed, and then climbed on top of me, straddling me at the waist. She grinned, batted her smokey eyes at me, and leaned her head back. And knowing what she wanted me to do, I slid one pinky into the mouth of her zipper and pulled down until her dress was completely open. She wriggled out of it, now astride me only in her collar and her boots. I began to touch her, rubbing her pert nipples with the balls of my thumbs, circling her waist with my hands.

I'd been correct in my fantasy assessment. She had no tattoos, no piercings other than the small silver hoops in her ears, which I licked and kissed when she bent down to me. Her white skin was striking against the black canopy above us and the black of her boots. I liked the dangerous feel of the vinyl boots against my own skin. It felt untamed, as if I were a pony and she my Mistress, taking me for a ride.

Others gathered around us. The music, which had been subtle during dinner, now shifted to the throbbing rhythm of rock and roll. *American* rock 'n roll. Aerosmith's "Dream On" was playing as my dream lover bent forward and kissed me, offering her ass to her husband, who stood behind her. I held her as Jean-Pierre fucked her. I kissed her raspberry-hued lips, licked the rise of her cheekbones, pressed my mouth to her smooth forehead. I stroked her hair, wrapped it around one hand as Daniel likes to do with mine, pulled and made her bring her face down to me.

Even as she kissed me, she arched her back so that her husband could get in deep. She wrapped her arms around my neck and held onto me as he impaled her with his cock. I moved with his rhythm, felt her body press against mine and rock with the force of his thrusts. I didn't look around for Daniel, sensed that he was close by, watching, approving. Claudia's husband pushed her forward, joining us on the bed until his hands were on either side of my head, the three of us merged into one wild creature. He spoke halting English, his breathing coming hard and fast, "She likes you. Claudia likes girls, she likes guys, she likes everyone. Don't you, Claudia?"

My baby mewed, like a kitten. Her husband speeded up the ride, fucking her ravenously and then slowing, slowing, and pulling out of her. He stood above us, still jerking his cock, milking it until he sprayed his come over her naked back. Daniel, at my side now, was quick to rub that lotion into Claudia's skin, to croon to me as he did so, "You liking this, baby? Your wish coming true?"

I grinned at him over her head, still holding her, not needing to respond. She and I stayed sealed together for a moment, and then Claudia murmured something and her man decoded the words for me. "Take her into the bathroom. Wash her, bathe with her."

I didn't need any other instructions. The club's bathroom is unisex and it's located along one side of the dance floor. A high-tech fantasy creation, the room boasts black-painted stalls, chrome sinks, and a shower walled in on three sides with glass, but open on the fourth. No door. No curtain. There were couples grinding beneath the silver disco ball, and Claudia and I made our way through them to the shower.

Some of the patrons had watched our escapade on the bed. Others seemed oblivious, but noticed us immediately when they saw Claudia, naked save for her boots, moving in sultry dance steps across the floor. Her image was reflected in the mirrors on the walls, and I saw people turn to stare, to try and find the real Claudia and not the reflection as we disappeared into the bathroom. A few lovers followed us. Claudia and I were sending off signals that were difficult to ignore.

Black tiles framed more mirrors above the bank of sinks. Claudia leaned against one wall and watched as I removed my rumpled dress, my panties, garters, heels, and hose. Then she stripped off her own boots and collar, took my hand, and entered the shower with me.

Inside the glass shower, we turned on the multiple shower heads and began to wash each other. There were bars of honey-scented soap and I lathered up with the sweet-smelling suds and then ran my hands over Claudia's naked body. Her skin grew slippery with the soap and water, and she pressed against me, slid into me, pushed me back against one glass wall. I looked over her shoulder, saw Daniel standing in the opening of the shower, watching. I called out for him to join us, but he shook his head, satisfied with being in the audience instead of partaking in the pleasure.

He motioned, like a film director, for me to kiss my newfound girlfriend. Holding her in my soapy embrace, I dug my fingers into her thick, wet hair, met her slick lips with my own. She kissed me back, then reciprocated the body-washing, lathering my breasts, my thighs, between my legs. She dropped the soap and neither of us thought to pick it up. I was lost in the heat of the shower and the heat of her mouth. I turned our bodies, pressed her back against one of the walls and kissing her pouty lips, the hollow of her neck, her breasts. She was mooning the dance floor with her lovely, pale asscheeks, and it drew even more faces into the opening of the shower.

The steam from the shower made me feel thick and hot, but the glass walls were cool and comforting. Claudia took control, turning me around again, my back to her this time. I was happy to let her take charge, to let my brain go on autopilot and my body swim in the need to do what she wanted me to. She pressed the flats of my palms against the glass and began to rub her body along my back. Then she went down on her knees on the wet tile floor and began probing me with her tongue, losing her fingers in my pussy and her curious tongue in my asshole. I gripped for purchase on the walls, but found nothing. I looked back over my shoulder for Daniel, but couldn't see him.

Claudia moved between my legs, turning her body so that her mouth found my clit and her fingers were now spreading my asscheeks. Her tongue mimicked the rhythm of the rock music pouring in from the dance floor. Now, Led Zeppelin playing "D'yer Mak'er." Claudia's mouth took me higher, her knowledgeable tongue, her fingers tickling my asshole. And then I heard my husband's voice, felt his cock pressing there, felt Claudia continuing with her tapping on my clit, and I started to moan. I ran my fingers through Claudia's wet hair, curling from the steam and the heat. I pressed my cunt forward, thrusting with my hips against her mouth as Daniel fucked my asshole hard and savage.

The soap on my body was the only lubrication he needed. He grabbed onto my shoulders and moved his hips back and forth, leaving the head of his cock in my ass, but rocking the shaft in and out. I was finding it hard to breathe. I looked down and saw Claudia's eyes locked on my face, her lips pursed around my clit. Daniel's body continued in its easy rhythm, the feel of his intruding cock making my heart beat faster, but the force of it welcomed by my body. Having Claudia working my clit relaxed me enough to really enjoy Daniel fucking me there. Usually, I need him to talk to me while he takes my back door. I need him saying things like, "Aren't you a naughty girl, liking it this way?" I need him to paint some sort of picture, some fantasy scenario, ass-fucking me as a way to show his power. Now, I only needed the real feeling of Claudia's mouth bringing me outrageous pleasure, and the knowledge that our act was being witnessed by a crowd of excited couples.

As I neared climax, Claudia's husband moved into the shower, standing close to me, deciphering things his wife didn't even have the time to say. "She wants you. She wants to see you come." I granted her wish before I could even think about it, my body throbbing, my heart beating so hard I could hear it in my ears. "She wants you to make her come..." he continued, while I was thinking "Of course, of course, now it's her turn," and quickly Daniel was pulling out and I was on the tiled floor with Claudia, turning in a sixty-nine, burying my face into her shaved pussy. I looked up once and saw that both Daniel and her husband were stroking themselves, and that Jean-Pierre had not even taken his clothes off, was standing in the spray of the shower, drenched totally, enthralled.

Claudia didn't let up with her tongue. Even though I'd already come, she seemed devoted to making me climax again. I did my best to please her, lapped at her pussylips, found her clit between my teeth and nipped at it. But no matter what I did, she just kept working me and her body showed no sign of reaching her ultimate peak.

Finally, her husband bent on his knees and said, "Roll over. You go on the bottom, let Claudia be on top."

I maneuvered our bodies as he said, never relinquishing her

pearl from between my lips. As soon as we were situated, I heard the sound of skin hitting skin. My body responded instantly, pushing up at Claudia's mouth, drenching her with the juice of my cunt. I love the sound of a spanking. Claudia's husband continued to smack her wet, naked ass while I worked her jewel, and between the two of us, we quickly had her body trembling with a powerful climax. Daniel, watching the festivities, shot his load against the glass of the shower and Jean-Pierre followed a beat later, coming on his wife's well-heated ass.

On shaky legs, we rinsed off a final time, then stepped aside and dried off, Daniel holding a towel out for me as soon as he'd gotten back into his clothes. The sweet hostesses were at our sides, giving Jean-Pierre a robe to wear, leading us to the bar as if we were celebrities.

Over champagne, Jean began telling us more about himself. But especially about Claudia. "She needs a little spank in order to come, a little shock of pain," he said. "She likes the rest. Claudia likes everything. But she needs that spark to get her over the top."

"Katrina, too," my husband said. "But your wife captivated her. She lost herself in Claudia's beauty."

I could tell Claudia understood because she blushed—the first time I'd seen her do that. Jean-Pierre continued. "You're the only other couple we've ever seen here who spanked." I looked up at him, startled, but he went on. "Last year, almost exactly this time. Downstairs." He spoke directly to Daniel. "We watched very attentively as you gave your wife a spanking. We've been coming back each Saturday since then."

Daniel grinned at Jean-Pierre. "I told her, but she wouldn't believe me. It always pays to get people's attention."

Games People Play
by Isabelle Nathe

You never know what's going to happen when you go out with Molly. She likes to be in charge, to set a mood and carry it through. So on Saturday night, when my best friend called and said to meet her at her apartment, I agreed without question. When Molly makes decisive statements, I rarely argue. It's how she's gotten me into the strip clubs out near the airport, specifically to *Meow, Meow Pussycat*, the one geared to lesbians. It's how I once ended up doing Tequila Body Shots with three very attractive strangers, knocking back the liquor, licking the salt off warm skin, and sucking the lime out of my new acquaintance's peony-lipsticked mouth. And it's how our picture appeared on the cover of an L.A. weekly paper for a piece about lesbians who were hip before people like Melissa, Ellen, and Chastity made it hip to be a lesbian.

But I had no idea what was on Molly's mind this evening. All she'd said when I arrived was this: "You won't believe what I have in store for you tonight." And now she seemed secretive and pleased with herself, which made me unbelievably nervous. I'm a shy sort of girl, myself. Shy, with a dirty mind. Was Molly going to make us enter a wet T-shirt contest? Or buy us red-eye tickets to Vegas? What was her plan? I stood in her bathroom, looking at my reflection, wondering whether I'd have the stamina to keep up with her tonight.

"What are you thinking?" Molly called from the bedroom. I turned to look over my shoulder at her. She was sprawled on her back on the bed, doing her best to zip herself into a pair of unbelievably tight jeans.

"Why don't you put on something comfortable?"

"These *are* comfortable, once I get them on," Molly groaned, "and that's not what you're thinking is it? That I should dress in a sack? If it is, I want you to lie to me and make something up."

"I was actually thinking that I look washed out," I announced, not willing to tell her my real worries about what her secret plans.

"All you need is some sexy lipstick." I watched as Molly inhaled deeply, got the zipper the rest of the way up, then stood and admired herself in the mirror across from the bed. Her ample ass looked divine in the denim. She grinned at me in the mirror as she gave herself a few light pats on the rear, then turned to poke through her jewelry box on the dresser. "You know where it is, Sidra. Top drawer on the left."

I pulled out the drawer to inspect Molly's collection, or, really, the evidence of her obsession. There were at least fifty tubes inside the drawer, all stacked neatly with their labels facing toward me. I didn't know where to start. Glancing at the bottoms of the lipstick tubes, I read the names to myself: Vamp, Obscene, Jezebel, Flirt. At least Molly is consistent in her choices.

"Grab the one in the cobalt blue case. It's called Cranberry Cocktail." I fumbled around until I found it. Of course, Molly had chosen a darker color for me than I normally would have, but when I put it on I discovered I liked it, getting into the look of myself staining my lips a deep ruby hue. I felt Molly approaching, and I turned to look at her for approval. She stood in the doorway, staring at me. "Is it too dark?" I asked.

"Did you know that women in ancient Egypt wore blue-black lipstick? I mean, like 6,000 years B.C."

"How do you come up with facts like that?"

Molly shrugged. Her shoulder-duster earrings swung back and forth. "I don't know. Lipstick trivia interests me. If they ever had a cosmetics column on *Jeopardy*, I'd win hands down. Anyway, the Egyptian women would think you look too pale; *you* think you look too dark. Call it a draw, and let's go."

She took a step toward me, dug her fingers through my hair, then pressed her lips firmly against mine. I leaned back against the porcelain sink, startled, my heart racing. She smelled of Chanel Number Five and talcum powder. Her hair tickled my cheeks and

I thought of putting my hands around her and pulling her even closer to me, of opening my lips to meet her tongue with mine, of sliding my lips down to the hollow of her neck and licking her there, biting her. Before I could do any of these things, Molly quickly backed away from me, slid her lips together, and glanced at herself in the mirror. "We'll both wear the same color," she said, and then registering my surprise, added, "Can you think of a sweeter way to put on lipstick than kissing it from a friend?"

I just shrugged. Molly's best feature is her ability to surprise. She is known for being daring. It's why her shyer friends, myself included, are pulled to her. And I wondered, excitement building inside me, what Molly would find for us to do tonight. As she reached for her purse, I noticed the pair of handcuffs hanging casually from the strap, but I thought it best to ignore them. Sometimes, all Molly needs is an opening to change the entire course of an evening.

Still, once she'd kissed me, couldn't I have guessed where she was headed? Was I that dense? I don't know why I couldn't have figured out her plans, but I didn't.

"Molly—" I started, uncertainly. I like to be prepared. It is one of my main quirks. I always need to know what's going to happen. This odd character flaw explains why I quiz friends about movie plots before heading to the cinema, why I can't make it through a mystery without flipping to the back of the book and reading the ending. Now, I had nothing, no inkling as to what was going on in Molly's X-rated mind.

"On the bed, Sidra." She tilted her head toward her brass bed which was covered with a shiny, satin comforter and mounds of multi-colored velvet pillows. Then she continued to stalk forward, like a cat, making me walk backwards until I bumped into the edge of her mattress and sat down. "Lie on your back with your hands over your head," she commanded. Just the sight of those silvery cuffs in Molly's hands made my pussy throb. I could imagine what the metal would feel like against my skin, what it would be like to have Molly in charge. Doing all the things she wanted to—and all the things I wanted her to do. But I needed her to vocally tell me, to spell it out before I acquiesced.

"What are you doing, Molly?" I whispered. "I mean, what are you going to do?"

"I'm going to fuck you," Molly explained, as if it were the most normal thing in the world for one best friend to seduce another. As if I were a little bit slow not to have figured this out for myself.

It had literally been years since Molly and I were an item. I was sort of interested in what it might be like to sleep with her. More than interested, the looks she gave me were making me hot. I could feel my heart beating, focused on that sensation as I stared at what Molly was holding in her hands.

"But why do you need the handcuffs?"

"That's the twenty-thousand dollar question," she said, smiling, "isn't it?"

As it turned out, Molly didn't *need* the handcuffs at all. She wanted them. There's a big difference in the world of bedroom play. I got the feeling that she would be perfectly adept at making love without toys, but the addition of extra paraphernalia added to her excitement. And this added to mine. Naked and captured to her bed with the cold steel cuffs around my wrists, I waited for her to join me. For those few moments, I wondered whether Molly was going to peel off the pants she had worked so hard to get into. Or would I be the only nude player in this scenario?

For once, I didn't ask. It felt as if I were in a dream, and I didn't want to ruin the magic of it. Yes, I like to know the endings, but I suddenly thought that maybe this was something I should work harder to change. Perhaps if I let myself go without knowing how a situation would wind up, I would have more fun during the actual experience. So I spent my time staring at Molly, seeing her in a different way than usual. More than my sexy best friend, now my sexy bed partner. But when would she stop staring at me and join me under the sheets?

She took her time, sitting on the edge of the bed and running her long crimson nails up and down the skin on the insides of my calves. This odd tickling sensation was entirely unique. I shivered each time her fingertips found out virgin territory.

"For years I've wanted to..." Molly started, now bending on the edge of the bed to kiss where her fingers had been mere moments before. Oh, I would melt. The feel of her warm, wet tongue on me had me straining against the handcuffs, which I'm sure was exactly what Molly had hoped for.

"Wanted to what?" I managed to whisper.

Molly didn't move her mouth from my skin when she spoke, which made it difficult for me to understand her answer. I repeated the question, and she removed her lips from me for a second, murmuring, "Wanted to taste you again...Candy."

Molly has called me that since senior year in high school when I'd had a thing for cherry lollipops. I'd always sucked one during English comp, and Molly had thought it was a cute habit. Turned it into a nickname. At least, that's what I'd originally thought. Because, as I said, this wasn't the first time Molly and I had been bedmates. It was the second.

On our last day of summer before starting college, she had come to my house to say goodbye, a bouquet of red cherry suckers in one of her hands. We'd gone up to the attic together, to an old sofa, and she had unwrapped one of the lollipops, licked it to get it nice and wet, and then slid it between my legs. Then she'd gone back and forth between licking me and sucking the lolly. I'd ended up coated with the sweet, sticky juices and so had Molly. As we'd climaxed together, she'd whispered, "I knew you'd taste like candy between your legs."

But why had it taken us so many years to try again? Molly explained now as she continued stroking me. "We were never free at the same time. You were with Toni, then Michelle, then Brenna. I was with Simone, then Georgia...."

She'd left out a few names, but I realized that she was right. When one of us was free, the other almost always had a girlfriend. And vice versa. Now, Molly continued her licking games up my body.

"But I can't wait any more," she sighed. "It's been too long. I really need to have your flavor on my tongue."

I couldn't have fought her if I wanted to, and I didn't want to. I just lay back and savored the moment as Molly brought her pouty lips to my delta of Venus, spread my nether lips with her fingers, and went to work. Or play. Or whatever you call it when your best friend goes down on you. And oh could she go down. Molly knew all the tricks, the special make-it-last tricks that you only learn after years of cohabitating with women. She pressed the flat of her tongue against my clit, firmly, until I groaned as I felt the first flicker of sexual fire burn through me. Then she left my clit alone completely and made darting circles around it until I arched my hips on the bed, trying to connect more firmly with her mouth.

This was why she had chosen to use the cuffs. They gave me a little room for action, but mostly left her in charge, which was exactly how Molly liked it. I realized at some point that she was still dressed, while I was nude, and that made me wetter still. Molly was intent on bringing me pleasure, in the slowest way possible, stretching it out until my whole body seemed to vibrate.

But finally, she seemed to want to feel my skin with her skin. And she stood and stripped, losing her clothes much more quickly than it had taken for her to put them on. Naked save for her long earrings, lying on the bed next to me, her pale skin seemed to glow, like the inside of a seashell. So white that it had a sheen to it. Unlike all of those tanned L.A. starlets, her body seemed purer for the lack of color.

I wished my hands were free so that I could touch her. But Molly didn't seem to mind, getting her body next to mine, caressing me with her skin. She arched her back, rubbed herself on me, worked in a way that made me think of a panther, stalking along the mattress toward me. As she moved up the bed, I stopped thinking and lost myself in the feel of her, the scent of her, the warmth of her body on mine. But when she moved to the side of the bed to kiss me, I looked down and saw that her cranberry lipstick was smeared along my lower belly. This is what made me come. Lipstick kisses on my skin, prettier than anything I'd ever seen before.

I threw my head back and let the swells of pleasure break over me, burst inside me like the surf pounding against the Santa Monica shore. They shook my body from the inside out, took me away and then gently, slowly brought me back down again. Into Molly's loving arms.

This evening, for all my fears of what she had in store for us, her plans had involved nothing but her, me, and a bed. Nothing else was needed.

The House of the Rising Sun
by M. Christian

Sunset: hot day melting into warm night. Amina stood, watching the shadows lengthen, feeling a heavy breeze pass her by—the hard iron balcony rail a stiff weight across her belly.

For a while she just looked at the people walking along the street below, calmly following their progress as they went wherever they were going. Not for the first time since Stanley had left her, she wanted to be one of them—any of them. A pair of Greek sailors; a young black man in threadbare jeans and a stained T-shirt, pedaling a wobbling, squeaking bicycle; a tourist couple in their pressed whites, standing out in their catalog-bought profiles; a fat man who didn't walk as much as slowly swim through the heavy sunset atmosphere, his legs seemingly linked by some internal arrangement to his fat arms swinging rhythmically by his side.

Many went by—till the sun had dropped behind the filigreed rooftops, and the street lamps started to, at first, glow then burn brightly—but she sadly remained herself.

Finally, the night touched, hinted at, becoming cool, so she turned away from the iron curlicues of the balcony and walked across the small boarding-house room to robotically turn the antique light switch by the door. Yellow light snapped down through a dirty, cracked ceiling fixture, bathing the room in harsh realism: sink stained with a rusty high-water mark, mirror above cracked with an angry bolt, wooden floorboards that had been worn not into a smooth sheen but rather a broken and splintered forest. Wallpaper covered the walls, a tawny rainbow of mildew, and where it didn't it curled away from the soft plaster in stiff tubes and torn twists.

"Bathroom's down the hall, girl; that's why you be gettin' this one so cheap," the manager had said. A polished noir Buddha, she'd sat, rocked back on a low stool by the front door. A simple white dress, all lace and tiny red stitching, covered her great body. She was a momma, like a primordial soft bosomy comfort made into a breathing person. As she spoke, she'd cooled herself with a fan lettered with a gospel hymnal—too slow to deliver a good breeze, but too fast for Amina to see what it said. "But you be gettin' a sink, so you ain't bein' completely uncivilized."

Amina hadn't argued, and yet hadn't agreed, either: the red brick building across the street from the iron pickets of the cemetery had neither been her destination or even a way point. She had been walking since dawn, a shocked somnambulation that had started with Stanley's note on the kitchen table, and ending with this big black woman calling to her: "Here, girl; rooms for a tired lookin' lady."

Money had been exchanged. How much Amina didn't care. Not many thoughts inhabited her mind during that long walk, and even after she'd climbed the stairs under the simply lettered sign: Rising Sun. Only a few thoughts had managed to make themselves known to her as she'd leaned over the balcony—wishes to be anyone but Amina Robinson.

Then, as the sun set and the not-hot, but-warm night had started, she thought a few more. Not words, really, just a cool rationalization: she'd not brought anything with her. No razors, no gun, not even some pills. She was only two floors up, too low to jump. The ceiling fixture didn't look strong enough to support her, even if she had anything like a rope. The mirror was obvious, razor-edged cracks promising—even without a handy bathtub.

In the end, she retreated to the mildew-sink of the too-soft bed, old springs complaining as she settled into it: not avoiding the escape she so desperately wanted, but rather not wanting to face even her fractured reflection.

Amina sat on the bed for a long time. Listening with half an ear to the architectural mumblings of the old building: the hissing of water through pipes, the rolling creeks of footsteps next door and up above, the flapping of the shade in the open window.

Like a toothache she couldn't help tonguing, she replayed Stanley—hurting herself with his absence. Each act—the last fight, the daisies he'd brought home from work one day, the way he'd looked at her when she undressed in front of him, the color of his nipples, his laughter—seemingly to press harder down on her shoulders. She cried, after a time, but her tears were long since used up.

She couldn't go on. She knew that, felt the truth of it somewhere down deep inside herself, but—still—she sat on the edge of that bed in the House of the Rising Sun and did nothing, except weep without tears.

Night: warm darkness pushed back by street lights, diluted by flickering advertisements. The sounds of passersby seemed louder, as if the sunlight of only a few hours before had done its own kind of pushing back, their volume increased by its absence. Now free, their voices and the sounds of their cars, bikes, and trucks echoed up into the small room.

Amina stood and went to the window, intending to close it. She stopped, though, in mid-stride. What did it matter? she thought to herself in sentiment if not in those exact words; I won't be able to hear anything very soon.

Then she did. Hear something, that is: a knock—thunderclap, pistol shot loud in the small room—and a voice: small, quavering, weak, helpless. "Hello," someone said from the other side of her door. "Hello? Can you hear me?"

She didn't have to. Still, she did: turn, walk to the door, slip the cheap chain, turn the knob, and open it just so much.

"Thank god, I thought someone wasn't in here." She was small, young—maybe 20 to Amina's 30, with hair as straight as dried pasta and as yellow as polished gold. Freckles dotted her pale cheeks, and her eyes were puffy and swollen from tears. "Please, can I come in—please?"

She didn't need to, but Amina did: open the door wider.

Stumbling over the first words in many hours, "S-sure" sounded like gravel pouring out of a coffee can.

"Thank you, oh thank you—" the young girl said, hunching down and moving quickly into the room. Then she turned, and before Amina could do anything, had wrapped her thin, surprisingly warm, arms around her.

Wet tears seeping through her dress, onto her shoulder, Amina's arms moved without her. The girl was so slight, so small, putting her arms around her was like hugging a doll.

"I just—I just didn't want to be alone," the girl said. Then she repeated, as much to herself as to Amina: "I just didn't want to be alone."

Amina patted her warm back, feeling—distantly—the knots of her spine and the planes of her shoulder blades. "I'm here," Amina said, without really feeling like she was.

"Can I ... can I stay with you for a while?" the girl said, pushing herself back just enough to look up into Amina's eyes.

Amina still wanted to leave, just not be ... there or anywhere else. But the girl's eyes, tugged at her, needed her. She didn't want to stay—in that room, in this world—but she also couldn't leave this sad, lonely girl, either.

Midnight: the darkness still warm, the sounds of sunset and early night chased away by the weight of hours. Twelve, it seemed was too deep, too black, to allow anything but a single wandering drunk who tried to sing—and failed—a song Amina didn't recognize.

Under the blankets, they were warm. How they'd gotten there seemed so quick as to be part of a half-performed dance. One step then another: "I just don't want to be alone anymore. Please, I just don't want to be alone." Then, "Thank you, thank you for opening the door. Thank you for being here." Her sobs had turned to shivers, and between her sobs she'd managed to slip, "Please, hold me."

And so, in bed. Curled around each other under the thin blankets against a turgid breeze—shivering, ever so slightly until their mingled heat stilled the tremors.

Amina didn't speak. Instead, she stroked the young girl's yellow hair—a soothing motion that seemed to come from somewhere deep inside herself. She thought about saying something, the first real thoughts she'd had all day, but didn't. Words wouldn't have been enough—so, instead, she just stroked the young girl's hair.

The girl, though, spoke—or rather mumbled sleepily into her shoulder: "I don't want to be alone anymore—don't want to be alone. Hold me, please, hold me. Don't want to be alone anymore...."

Sleep started to tug at them, then pull in earnest. Before she was even aware of it, Amina's eyes closed and—to the soft, rhythmic breathing of the young girl, she drifted off. She dreamed of Stanley, of a time when the two of them had rolled around on their tiny bed in the back of their little house. It was like a slippery body memory, the touch of Stanley's rough hands on her thighs, the weight of his hips on hers, the slight tang of beer on his breath, the slight burning of his stubble as they kissed. The way his sharp toenails occasionally grazed her ankles.

From this she drifted up, floating away from the dream and back into that warm, dark room. The girl, invisible under the blankets, was molded on top of her—the gentle weight of her small body pressing lightly down, pushing Amina into the thin mattress. One of the girl's hands cupped Amina's right breast, her fingers calmly stroking the sides, delicately pinching her nipple.

Stanley had been a ferocious lover, a two-armed, two-legged thrust needing something to penetrate. When his lips found her nipples, Amina usually paid for this nurturing need of his with an even more vigorous than usual fuck—as if he was forcing his prick through herself and into his own weakness. A fuck like that was more a demonstration of his force than a need to come. After a time, Amina had feared his chapped, thin lips near her breasts and had taken to wearing at least a T-shirt to bed, and sometimes even a bra.

Sometime during the night the temperature had risen—and buttons had come unbuttoned. The girl's lips were too soft, too delicate: it was as if a hint, and not firm reality, was kissing—then sucking—Amina's nipples. The ghostly memory of Stanley's rough lips, flashed through her mind—then faded with a great surging wave of tingling pleasure. Even the deep reflexes of fear that usually accompanied any kind of contact with her nipples was stilled by the loving touch of the girl's gentle lips. With the wave, the swelling bloom of her body's response—nipples knotted, heart beating faster, breath shallower, muscles tightening, cunt liquefying—Amina found Stanley fading for the first time. A small tongue ringed her crinkled tips, and against her will, she found herself arching to meet the accompanying gentle suction.

It wasn't so much a girl's lips and tongue on her body—for Amina didn't really think of her in that way. In the darkness of the room, with the hole that Stanley's cruelty and departure had opened in her, it was just contact. Someone had looked down, saw the fragile, broken woman at the bottom, and had extended a hand down. Lips didn't matter as much as the thought of being seen, and desired—who it was incidental to that fact.

Distantly, through the hot, heavy haze of the girl's breath between kisses, between sweet nibbles, between sucks, Amina caught the falling bass note of a ship's horn sounding on the river. The reminder of the heavy waters of the Mississippi, the still-turgid atmosphere of the night air, made it seem as if she were floating in bath water—buoyed by the girl's touches on her body. The sucking, yes, but also her thin fingers dancing along her sides, the curves of her heavy breasts, the tension of her thighs, the gentle quakes of her calves seemed to lift Amina up, hold her above the bed, above even the sad exterior of the House of the Midnight Sun.

Squeezing her eyes shut against a sudden sharp peak of excitement, young teeth grazing her so-tight nipples as the girl's fingers playfully pinched at the underside of her tits, brought stars to Amina's eyes—completing the illusion of flight. Deep into a warm night, hanging above a vibrant tapestry of blue and purple starbursts, she floated on the girl's tender desire.

When those hands fell to the inside of her thighs, Amina parted them without a thought—save to be propelled higher into that starry canopy and away from the harsh earth, away from small rooms in run-down hotels, away from the pain of breathing, away from the pain of loneliness.

The first kiss was a lighting tear across that velvet darkness, a quick flash of desire that made Amina grit her teeth and whistle a breath. The first lick, the girl's tongue cautiously starting at the top of Amina's already wet cunt—just shy of her throbbing, pulsing clit—was a shivering rush through her body, a chiming that seemed to race through her. Toes to nose, Amina's body tensed and relaxed, tensed and relaxed to the accompanying strokes of the girl's strong, stiff tongue along her labia.

She crashed—down, down, down, through the ceiling, wham! into her body. Amina was a woman, on a smelly mattress, under a thin blanket, in a dive somewhere near the French Quarter, with a girl she'd didn't know. Her legs were spread, her nipples were hard, and her cunt was very wet. She almost brought those legs closed to keep the girl away from her and the shimmering pleasure she was delivering. She even tensed in preparation, lifting a hand—feeling it drag and catch at the scratchy blanket—to put it on the girl's head, and half-formed the words no, please. But she stopped, hand only raised, legs only slightly tensed, words completely unspoken.

At first she didn't know what it was. Later, in the morning and days beyond, Amina would look back at that moment with some sadness (too long) and much joy (looking forward to more)—but there in that little hotel, in the middle of a warmish night, it was just good. It was the best kind of good, a whole, pure, brilliant, good.

The moan escaped Amina's lips without permission, escaping from tension and loneliness—a long struggle that made its release all the more intense. Soon, the moan turned to gasps, which evolved into sweet murmurs—cresting once, twice, and more, many more times in more sharp cries, more deep moans.

What the girl was doing was a mystery. But Amina didn't care. She was there, in that sad hotel, on that warm night, under that cheap blanket, and she didn't care. She was desired, and—best of all—she was loved.

They came even faster after that, as if the way had been opened and the coming flowed through that opening in herself. With each, her liberation released her body, and her hands rubbed the girl's head between her legs, stroked her tiny ears, and allowed her legs to squeeze—ever so slightly.

How many was a mystery—one of many. In the end, she slept—the opening and the outpouring exhausting her. As she slept she dreamed, but on waking she couldn't remember anything about it—except she hadn't been alone. Stanley hadn't been there, but she hadn't been alone.

When she awoke, hard morning sunlight beating through the open window, the girl was gone. The front door was closed, but just barely: a narrow seam of hallway showed between the thin wood and the jam. Amina's dress was twisted and bunched. Standing quickly, she turned it, buttoned it, and smoothed it where it had crept up the cheeks of her ass.

Then she opened the door wider. The corridor was empty—quiet except for the muffled conversations of static-laced televisions talking to themselves. As she walked, then trotted, then ran towards the stairs, she wanted to call out, to cry the girl's name ... and felt a deep tug down inside herself when she realized that she didn't know it.

The manager, the Buddha momma was outside, as if the black woman had not moved from her seat near the front door. As Amina trotted down the threadbare hall, the woman kept her rhythmic fanning—steady and undisturbed.

The street was just waking, slow pedestrians and the unearthly quickness of those used to the early hours. Faces approached and the silhouettes of bodies retreated but, standing on the narrow street, none of them was the girl.

"Excuse me," Amina panted, turning back to the big black woman, "but did you see a young woman go out? She was blond, thin—blue eyes ...."

"Ah, girl," momma said, smiling—a pure beaming light of

cheekbones, bright eyes, and a shimmering smile, "she's gone, she is. Been here long enough, but she's had ta got back ta where she belongs."

"Please, I want to find her. Tell me where she is...?" Amina said, hunger panting her words, making them sharp and forced.

"Girl, she be where she always be. She be where she come from," momma said, smile never wavering as she snapped her hymnal fan shut with a clap of rattan and paper. "She be where she be loved. You just be needin' to be shown that she there, is all. Sometimes you just be needin' to be shown how to be there for yerself, how ta love yerself." With the fan, momma leaned slowly forward and tapped—one, two, three—Amina between her breasts, over her rapidly beating heart.

"If the lonely be bitin', you just look down here—" tap, tap, tap— "and know that she be there. She always be there, girl, when you be needin' ta love yerself."

The day was starting. The city waking and starting to move around them. Smiling, leaning forward, Amina kissed the black woman on the forehead. Then she slowly walked off into the beginning of a day—the girl staying with her, keeping her company, loving her, with every step.

In Progress
by J. Richards

I realize now that at the beginning Colette was simply taking things slowly, being easy on such a wild stallion as myself. She thought if she moved too fast she might scare me off and into the arms of another, less-focused Mistress. And she was right. Had she spooked me with constant discipline, with too-soon, too-hard punishment, I would have fled. But instead, she teased me, taunted me, until I found myself asking her for it. Begging her for it.

Standing in front of the refrigerator, reading over Mistress Julian's comments in a column cut from *Bad Girl*, feeling the heat and wetness start to flow at my core... that's when I began to understand the structure of a D/s relationship. Lowercase "s," always, head bowed, eyes lowered. Humble. I wasn't humble, clad in tight black stretch pants and a lycra running top, my hair a jumble of windswept curls, my cheeks flushed from my morning run. I wasn't humble as I poured my juice into one of our vintage jelly glasses and prepared to make a single slice of toast.

Humble means getting Colette's meal first, bringing it on a tray to her bedroom, serving her with head bowed and then asking, in my softest voice, if there is anything else I can get for her. Humble means sitting on my heels on the floor by the bed, shoulders back, body arched, waiting for her to choose to feed me a bite of her toast, a bit of her muffin, a sip of her juice.

No, I was not humble. I was wild and spirited, unbroken and untamed. But I was searching. My day-job, my real-world, my nine-to-five life is perfect for that type of personality—though I lie, it's never nine-to-five, it's all-consuming.

I'm an artist, fairly successful for one so young, my work shown in many of the downtown galleries and quite a few of the private, wealthier estates in our community. I have a luminous quality to my art, they say, I have a free-flowing hand, a lack of inhibition when it comes to paints and brushes and colors in tubes. I have no fear of light or dark, of shading, of muting, of brightness, of screaming.

On the canvas, that is.

But alone, in bed, with my Mistress, I am out of control, all over the place, my strokes too heavy or too light, my body contorting in a vain effort to find peace. I need control here, where I have none. My breathlessness of art does not serve me well. My constant moving, shifting and gliding, my colors as they burst free—each one a different shade, a different hue—these take me further from my goal, not closer to it.

Colette sees this all, and she knows, and she ponders the best way there is to rein in a free spirit without damaging the soul. Her blue eyes flash with ideas, with concepts, but she doesn't rush into anything. She would not have me destroyed, she would not have the filament that glows inside me damaged, she would only have me tamed, when I am in her arms in bed. She would only have me find the peace that I so crave.

I used to be envious of those who possess that peace. I used to talk to girls on the bus who ferry themselves from job to home to TV dinners without so much as a thought to art or life or pleasure or pain. They were the lucky ones, I thought, without the need inside them that burns inside me. The fire that causes me to toss and turn restlessly in my Mistress' embrace—the inner rage that never lets up, that never finds its mark.

Sometimes, I'd talk to them, asking what they did for fun, flirting casually, easily, searching for the answer. Why were they so different? They seemed like creatures in a zoo, under glass, pinned down. I wanted to observe them, wanted to find out what was missing inside them that could enable them to enjoy watching soulless movies, empty TV, overly-bland theatrical performances. What was it? What was it?

Ah, maybe you've already guessed. It wasn't a lack in them, wasn't something they'd been born without, but something that I had been born with. Something that I had no control over, the heat, the fire, the need to create. And creating takes that extra bit and builds it up until it is a constant vein of life pulsing beneath the skin. You can't turn it on when you're in slump, you can't turn it off when you want to sleep. The paintings call you, the paintbrushes speak, the tubes of color wake you up.

Come and create, they whisper. Forget food. Forget sleep. Forget love. Forget life. Come and make things of us. We need freedom. You can give us that freedom.

Doomed, head bowed, my Mistress is my art. She calls to me and I go. She beckons me, and I am hers. I walk on heavy feet to the studio and open the door. The light is just right, streaming through the window in curtains of yellow and gold. The paintings stand against the wall, mocking me, howling at me: finish us! What do you think you're doing? Sleeping? No sleep. No time. You don't have enough time.

There is too much art in my head.

It must come out.

Colette knows this, she strokes the side of my face when I sleep, she kisses my lips and tastes the life there, she uses a cool rag to wash the drips of paint from under my nails. She bathes me. She feeds me. She keeps my outer-workings in healthy order so that someday, sometime, I may find peace.

No peace while those voices call to me.

Come to the studio, there are ideas here. You can let them out. You can be free of them.

The stallion inside me bucks up and raises its head. I moan and look at the clock. "It's too early," I say to no visible creature. "Too early to start work."

"No," those voices chide at once. "It's too late."

I pull on my robe and wander to the studio, opening the door and staring at my works-in-progress. They call to me, like hungry children, feed me, finish me, use yourself up to make us whole. I find strength as I begin to mix the paints, my palette a ray of sin and light, of dark and heat, of wet and dry. I do not think in terms of colors, do not know the names of the tubes, but, instead, the feel of them in my hand. How much of this one has been used up, how much of that. The crinkly metal that folds and condenses, that looks so strong, but, once empty, is weak and brittle.

I gather my strength and I begin to paint, the moonlight playing melodies on my ghostly form. The sound of my feet as I shuffle on the wood floor a rhythm that matches my heart.

Colette knows—her blue eyes appear on my canvas, watching— Colette knows, and she tries, so hard, to understand. But she is not one of the artists, the few, the chosen, the cursed. She is not one of us. But she tries, she comes to stand in the doorway of the studio, her nightgown hanging long and loose down her body, her hair a tangle of gold spun from straw. She watches me work, never speaking, never interrupting, and I know—in a split second of wisdom—that she is as envious of me as I am of her.

She is complete, she is finished. She will never be anything but who she is.

While I ... I am a work in progress.

Joining the Club
by Lisa Pacheco

I'm sure you've heard of the Mile High Club. Personally, I never saw the point. What's so cool about having sex in one of those miniature bathrooms? I wondered. Slammed against the mirror with your legs spread wide, trying to avoid plunging one foot in the neon-blue toilet water while keeping your ass out of the sink. I like comfort. I like plenty of room. I like to make noise.

But on our recent flight from New York to San Francisco, Sam and I found ourselves in a new predicament. We fell asleep, my head resting lightly on his shoulder, his strong arm wrapped firmly around my body. And once asleep, I began to dream.

Have you ever had a sex dream so real that you were certain the person you dreamed about must have shared it with you? This one was like that—an image of us from recent memory. Raw. Outta control. It was a vision of Sam fucking me on the hood of my car, my legs hooked over his shoulders. Staring down at me in the dimly lit parking garage, that greedy look filling his gray-green eyes, whisper-hissing, *"Like that? You like it like that?"* with each forward thrust.

"Yeah..."

"Oh, I know you do, my hungry one. I know all about you."

I stirred on the plane, feeling the flushed, embarrassed heat in my cheeks, the wetness between my legs from just a dream. Then I looked at him. His eyes were open, watching me.

"You're beautiful when you sleep."

I smiled, then told him about my dream, and he leaned back in the seat and said, "I wish we were somewhere we could turn that into a reality." I checked my watch. We had three more hours of flight time.

"Do you want to...?" he finally asked, motioning toward the rear of the jet. And there it was—I suddenly understood the whole concept of doing it on a plane. I unbuckled my seat belt and walked back to the lavatories. He followed.

When you hear people bragging about their indoctrination into the Mile High Club, they don't usually mention the amazing difficulty it can be to get two people into one bathroom. We are both full-grown adults and airplane rest rooms were built for munchkins. Despite the close quarters, Sam pushed me into the lavatory, followed me in, and shut the door behind us.

In a flash, I was up on the rim of the sink, back against the mirror, legs splayed—forgetting all about my previous misgivings. I hiked my black skirt as high as it would go and slid my cream-colored panties to the side. Sam was ready, pressing forward, cock plunging inside me.

And *that's* when the turbulence hit. The little red warning light flashed, commanding us to return to our seats. The pilot's manly drone insisted that our belts be buckled. Sam kept right on going. It was like taking a ride on the top of a washing machine, the motion of the plane, the delicious friction of his body against mine. Disregard everything I said about the tiny compartment, about the foul blue water, about the sink. My breath caught in my throat, my hands gripped the edge of the steely counter for leverage. My mind was consumed entirely with want.

There was a knock on the door. "You have to return to your seat..."

"I'm not feeling well..." I hissed, my voice heavy and dark with urgency.

"Oh," she left it alone, not wanting to get involved.

"Ohhhh..." I murmured, echoing her. "That's right. *Yeah*, that's right."

Sam grabbed the back of my hair, lifting my face upward for a kiss. We tried, but missed, as the plane suddenly bucked and we were thrown against each other. Now I was pressed against him, feeling his hands cradling my ass, plunging me up and down on his rod. The red light continued to flash. The captain continued to speak over the intercom, describing exactly what was causing the pockets of rocking air. Didn't matter. Nothing mattered except the way it felt to be in Sam's embrace, the way the motion of the plane worked with the motion of our bodies.

Sam turned in a tight circle, so that his back was now against the rim of the sink and I was still in his arms. I could see my reflection in the mirror. My blue eyes glowed in the fluorescent light. My cheeks were rose-tinted, fever-flushed. My teeth bit hard into my lower lip, smearing what lipstick I still had on.

"Now," Sam said.

"...now." I breathed a harsh sigh of release, relief, as we came together. The vibrations worked to set me off, those, and the last wild jerks of the plane caught in a violent burst of air. Then, as the turbulence lessened, slowed, and the air become calm... so did I.

Sam set me gently down on the floor. Cautiously, he slid the door open and then quickly slipped out and closed the door. I re-latched it, cleaned up, and then joined him back at our seats. No one saw, but the flight attendant came to my side after a moment, handing me an extra air sick bag, with the words of caution, "Just in case...."

Killing the Marabou Slippers
by Molly Laster

They looked like any other innocent pair of bedroom slippers. But maybe they weren't quite so innocent. Maybe they knew what they were doing all along. You've seen the type—smug in their open-toedness. Willful in their daring high-heeled glory. Decadently trimmed with a bit of tender white marabou fluff on the front, just to get your attention.

I'd never owned shoes like these before. Sure, I'd seen versions of them in the Frederick's of Hollywood catalog, insolently positioned with toe toward the camera, daring the casual pursuer to purchase them. And I'd even drooled over such fantasy footwear when worn by my favorite forties screen stars: Myrna Loy. Claudette Colbert. Garbo. But those women had the clothes to go with the shoes—angel-sleeved nightgowns with three-foot trains, tight satin slips with plunging necklines. Such sexy slippers weren't meant for someone like me—a girl who owns plain white bra and panty sets, who wears Gap sweats to bed, whose one experience with a pair of black fishnets was a comedic disaster. What purpose could a pair of wayward shoes like these possibly have?

Still, when I caught sight of the immoral mules at a panty sale in San Francisco, I bought them. Even though they were a size eight and I'm a size six. Even though I found the very sight of them fairly wicked. Even though my own bedroom slippers at home were made of plaid flannel and had been chewed on repeatedly by my Golden Retriever puppy.

I simply thought Lucas would like them.

He did.

"I'm gonna fuck those shoes," he said when I pulled them from the silver mylar bag. "Sweetheart, those shoes are history."

I'd never seen him react like that to anything. My tall, handsome, green-eyed husband has a healthy libido. I definitely get my share of bedroom romping time. But as far as kinkiness goes, he has always appeared positively fetish-free. No requests for handcuffs. No need for teddies or "special" outfits to get him in the mood. No urgent trips to Safeway at midnight for whipped cream, chocolate sauce, and maraschino cherries.

"Put them on," Lucas hissed. "Now."

I kicked off my patent leather penny-loafers, pulled off my black stockings, and slid into the marabou mules. The white bit of fluff on the toes made the shoes look like some sort of pastry, a fantasy confection created just for feet. My red toenails peeked through the opening. *Dirty*, I thought. *Indecent.*

Lucas got on the floor and kissed my exposed toes, stroked the soft feathery tips of the shoes, then stood and quickly shed his outfit.

"They're bad," he said excitedly, positioning himself over my feet as if preparing to do push-ups. He's ex-military and has excellent formation for this activity—his body becomes stiff and board-like. The sleek muscles in his back shift becomingly under his tan skin. In this position, his straining cock went directly between the two mules.

"Oh, man," he whispered. "So bad they're good."

He went up and down over my shoes, digging his cock between them, dragging it over the marabou trim, sighing with delight when the feathers got between his legs. I could only imagine how those pale white feathers tickled his most sensitive organ.

"They're so soft," he murmured.

I'd been staring down at him, at his fine ass—clenching with each depraved push-up—at his strong back, the muscles rippling. Now, I looked straight ahead, into the full-length mirror across the room, taking in the total effect of our afternoon of debauchery.

I was fully dressed: long black skirt, black mock turtleneck, my dark hair in a refined ponytail, small spectacles in place. If you ended the reflection at my shins, you might have placed me for exactly what I am, an editor at an educational publishing company.

Below my shins, however, was Lucas, doing ungodly push-ups over my brand-new shoes. My slim ankles were bare, feet sliding slightly in the too-big marabou-trimmed mules. If you disregarded the shoes, and imagined Lucas moving in stop-frame animation, he might have been culled from a series of Eadweard Muybridge pictures. But with the shoes in place, and with Lucas's body moving rigidly up and down, this picture looked more like something from a fantastic pornographic movie.

I stared at our images and felt myself growing more and more aroused. My plain white panties were suddenly too containing. My skirt and sweater needed to come off. Arousal rushed through me in a shuddering wave. But I kept my peace—this wasn't my fantasy, wasn't my moment. It was Lucas's. All his.

He began speaking louder, first lauding the shoes, "Sweet, so sweet." Then criticizing the slippers as he slammed between them, "Oh, you're bad...bad."

I stayed as still as possible, watching in awe as Lucas, approaching his limit, arched up and sat back on his heels, his hand working his cock in double-time. Small bits of pure white feathers were stuck to the sticky tip of his swollen penis. More feather fluffs floated in the air around us.

"Give me one of the shoes," he demanded, and I kicked off the right slipper. One hand still wrapped around his cock, he used the other to lift the discarded shoe and began rubbing the tip of it between his legs, moaning and sighing, his words no longer legible, no longer necessary. Then, suddenly, as if inspiration had hit him, he reached behind his body with the shoe, poking the heel of it between the cheeks of his ass, impaling himself with the slipper while he dragged the tip of his cock against the shoe I still wore.

I watched closely as his breathing caught, as he leaned back further still and then came, ejaculating on the slipper before him, coating those naughty feathers with semen, matting the feathers into a sticky mess. Showing them once and for all who was boss.

When he had relaxed enough to speak, he looked up at me, a sheepish expression on his face. "Told you those shoes were history," he said, embarrassed. "Told you, baby, didn't I?"

I just nodded, thinking to myself: The death of an innocent pair of marabou slippers. What'd the shoes ever do to Lucas? Nothing but exist.

Lonesome Highway
by Christy Michaels

It started like any other night. I was backstage, waiting for the first savage beats of Nine Inch Nail's "Closer to God," the signal for the beginning of my set. The other girls usually pick something from the DJ's slush pile: golden oldies, 60's rock, the odd rap song. I bring my own CDs. New, edgy stuff they won't play on the radio. The manager always complains about my choice of music... but never about my dancing.

My costume that night was a crimson-and-white sequined micro-top over a blue star-shaped thong. Very patriotic. It had been a hot summer and my tan line consisted of a tiny white strip between my legs. When the music started, I pushed through the black velvet curtain, shook out my long platinum hair, and took the stage with a vengeance. I always like to start my set off with a bang and break a sweat before the music stops. Seductively, I leapt to the top of the brass pole, arched my back and slid slowly to the floor.

On the way down, I noticed *she* was here again. The cop with the coal-black hair. She sat behind a table at the end of the runway, her face in shadow, eyes invisible behind mirrored shades. She had a style that belied her profession; a sort of East Village street chic that bled right through the uniform. There was something about her that made my pussy ache.

I'd seen her in the club every Tuesday night for two months. She came late and usually left right after my set. This time, I was going to make her talk to me. As Trent Reznor roared my song's refrain, I worked my way over to her table and pulled the fabric of my top tight over my erect nipples. She lit a cigarette. I let the straps fall down my bare shoulders. She blew a plume of blue smoke into the darkness. I flung the glittering fabric through air. It fluttered like a bizarre insect and landed on the table in front of her. She held it to her face and inhaled, leaving the cigarette smoldering in the corner of her mouth.

I know all the ways to turn the heat up, but she was different from anyone I'd ever danced for. I dropped down on my knees on the carpeted floor and looked up at her with my best come-hither eyes.

Nothing.

I pushed my chest out, scooped a hand under each breast and rubbed the nipples until they were standing at stiff attention.

Nada.

Although my act wasn't having much effect on her, she was sure turning me on. Under the thong, my cunt was dripping wet. I just wanted to rip the thing off and push my freshly shaved pussy into her face. Instead, I crawled onto the table and knelt in front of her. To my surprise, her hand came up with a creased twenty-dollar note between the fingers.

"Nice dancing..." she said. Her voice was filled with ice, but somehow it made me hotter still. "What's your name?"

I couldn't remember. And then I didn't think my mouth would work to tell her. I licked my lips, staring at my reflection in her shades. Finally, I managed, "Casey."

"Nice dancing, Casey." Without changing her expression, she slid the bill into the band of my thong, letting her fingertips linger on the slippery edge of my pussy. An electric current shot straight up my spine. Another moment and I would have come right there in front of everyone. As it was, my song ended. I stumbled to my feet and rushed backstage.

Something dark, deep, and just a little bit scary was bubbling up inside me. I tossed my thong in my purse and threw on my black suede dress and pumps. Without bothering to put on panties, I grabbed my car keys and rushed out the back door. All I wanted was to get behind the wheel of my car and drive. A cherry-red '65 Vette is my priest, analyst, and best girlfriend all rolled into one. Any time something gets to me, I take it out on a lonesome highway in the dark and drive. The faster the better.

I raced out of the parking lot and left a patch of rubber where my tires hit the pavement. The highway was empty, not another car in sight. I hit the gas and the needle jumped... 80... 90... 100.... The pavement under my headlights passed in a blur, but I couldn't get her out of my head: the shiny black hair, mocking lips, faint smell of leather. My left hand dropped between my legs, two fingers dipping into the wetness of my pussy and sliding up over the swollen bud of my clit.

That's when the dark field behind me exploded with flashing red lights. I looked down at the gauge. 110-miles-an-hour. I skidded onto the shoulder and watched in my side mirror as the highway patrol car rolled up behind me. The driver's door opened and the officer got out. In the flare of the headlights, all I could see was a menacing silhouette walking toward my window. Then I heard a voice that made the butterflies in my belly do loop-the-loops.

"Put your hands on the wheel," she said. It was the voice of authority laced with the faintest undercurrent of mockery. *Her* voice.

I looked down and realized with a jolt that my hand was still between my legs and my dress was hiked up to my waist. I felt the blood rush to my face in embarrassment and arousal. My heart began to race. I'd been caught speeding *and* masturbating. In my state the first spells a suspended license, a stiff fine, and a night in jail. I had no idea what the penalty for the second would be.

"You know how fast you were going, little lady?" she asked, the mockery surfacing. A smile played at the corners of her pretty mouth.

"I'm sorry," I stammered. "I guess I was a little... distracted."

"Get out of the car."

Without bothering to adjust my clothes, I climbed out. The cool night air caressed my bare ass and I could feel my nipples stiffen under the leather of my dress. "Nice," she muttered under her breath as she led me back to the tail-end of the Vette. She spun me around in the blinding glare of her highlights and pushed me face down onto the trunk of my car.

"Head down and spread 'em!" she commanded.

Off balance, I spread my legs and leaned forward onto the trunk. Her gloved hands were immediately all over me, touching and probing. At the tops of my inner thighs, they stopped and lingered for a long moment before continuing down my legs. I shivered uncontrollably, feeling the familiar surge building toward a climax.

"Cold?" she asked.

"No," I whispered. "It's just that... I can't afford a ticket. Is there anything I can do to avoid that, Officer...?"

"McKennzie. And the answer is 'no.' I'm afraid I'm going to have to give you everything you've got coming to you," she answered. Then I heard the sound of leather whipping through belt loops and something heavy hit the gravel of the shoulder.

"You shoulda been good," she drawled. "Not out here drivin' fast. You've been naughty. Naughty girls get punished."

THWACK! The first blow came as a surprise, the thick leather of her uniform belt cutting into the bare cheeks of my ass and taking my breath away.

"Next time you're gonna be a good girl. Aren't you, Casey?" She brought the belt down a second time. I closed my eyes, picturing her belt on my bare ass in the headlights. Each blow was a turn-on; the sting a potent cocktail of pleasure and pain.

"Yes, Officer," I promised, wondering how many strokes she was going to make me take and not sure of how many I'd be able to stand. Then the whipping suddenly stopped, and I could feel her lips on my burning asscheeks as she kissed the welts.The tips of her fingers slid between my legs. "You're dripping wet," she observed in a husky voice.

"I can't help it," I whispered. "You make me want..."

She didn't let me finish. "Take off your dress," she ordered. I slowly pulled the flimsy piece of black suede over my head and stood naked in the headlights. She knelt inches from my pussy, pushed the lips open with her tongue, and began to lap my juices. In ecstasy, I reached up and stroked my nipples. They were harder than I'd ever felt them, jutting forward against my fingers. I pinched them between thumb and forefinger as the officer nipped my clit between her teeth. Just when I felt an explosion about to go off inside me, she spun me back onto the trunk of the car.

The next thing I felt was the cool, smooth tip of her nightstick. She used it to trace the surface of my inner thighs then slowly sank the first three inches into my cunt. "This is what happens to bad little girls," she murmured, plunging the wooden pole deeper inside me. I began to buck and moan. Every sound earned me a sharp spank on the ass. The more I cried out, the harder she spanked me until I was once again on the brink. That's when she pulled the nightstick out.

"I don't think I'm going to give you what you want just yet," she said. I knew better than to reply. She unzipped the trousers of her uniform and lowered her slacks. Then she grabbed me by the hair and pushed me on my knees before her. Her fist wrapped in my curly mane, she pulled my face hard against her pussy. I went to work licking and sucking, and her clit responded by growing thick and hard between my lips. I pushed three fingers deep inside her hot, slippery cunt and she started sliding up and down on them. Feeling her tense up, I moved my tongue faster and slid my middle finger up her ass. She started to shake and quiver, exploding in a full-body orgasm.

When the last spasm subsided, she looked down at me. Her eyes were unreadable. I started to tremble as she slid her pants back up, pulled me to my feet, then reached for her handcuffs and cuffed my hands behind my back. I felt the nightstick run up my leg and back into my pussy. She slid it in deep and began to fuck me nice and slow, rubbing my clit with her fingers. When she dropped to her knees and started to lick my ass, I almost lost it.

"Please..." I said, not knowing how to say what I wanted, but hoping she would understand. She did. She pulled the nightstick out of my pussy, moved it back to my asshole, and slid it in my back door. The feeling of being filled was so intense that I thought I was going to come on the spot. But then I heard the roar of a car approaching and instantly stiffened. *"We're going to get caught,"* I thought. *"But we can't get caught! She can't stop... not now...not yet!"*

Officer McKennzie ignored the car and started to lick my pussy as she plunged the nightstick deeper and deeper into my ass. I felt a mind-numbing orgasm building up inside me. She moved her tongue over my cunt faster and faster.

Out of nowhere, a second set of hands grabbed my tits and squeezed the nipples. A pair of full, warm breasts pressed against my bare back. The driver of the car was definitely female and she was getting off on me being fucked by the officer. That was enough to send me over the edge. I began to fuck the nightstick, sliding it as far into my ass as it would go. Officer McKennzie lapped up my juices, alternating her tongue and fingers in my pussy. I couldn't hold back any longer. My ass tightened around the nightstick as I rocked and moaned with pleasure.

When I was finished, she unlocked the handcuffs and I slid to the ground. I looked up and to my surprise discovered that the newcomer was another cop. She wore the same black leather boots and tight blue uniform as Officer McKennzie, but her shirt was open, revealing the voluptuous curves of her breasts. And she was taller, with wheat-colored hair captured in a ponytail. The two cops embraced and began to kiss. Staring at them together was magical; like witnessing the mating dance of two animals in the wild.

As I watched, they ripped the clothes off each other's bodies with untamed passion, kissing every curve and crevasse as if for the first time. When they were both naked, the blonde cop slid her hands under Officer McKennzie's ass and lifted her up onto the trunk of the car. She kissed and licked her nipples until they were fully erect, then moved down over her tan stomach to her sex. There she began to slowly move her tongue in circles over the tip of her clit, teasing ever so slightly.

Officer McKennzie's fallen flashlight lay on the gravel at my feet. It was a jumbo Maglite, as big around as my wrist. The blonde cop grabbed it and inserted the back end into Officer McKennzie's cunt. As she slid the black shaft in and out, she began to suck her partner's clit until she was bucking and moaning on the waves of her climax.

Without stopping to catch her breath, Officer McKennzie jumped down and threw the blonde cop onto the trunk. She looked over at me, issuing a silent command with her eyes. I crawled over and nuzzled the blonde cop's pussy. It was shaved smooth—just the tiniest wisp of pale hair at the very top. I stuck out my tongue and began to lap up her juices as Officer McKennzie pulled back her hands and snapped on the handcuffs.

She picked up the nightstick and slid it deep into her partner's cunt. Running my tongue over her swollen clit, I could feel her excitement build. When Officer McKennzie grabbed the flashlight and pushed it up the blonde cop's ass, her whimpering cries become wild shouts of abandon. She began rubbing her clit against my tongue so fast that I knew she couldn't last another minute. I started to suck the tip of her clit between my moist lips. She tensed up, then pushed her ass back hard on the flashlight and screamed as her body exploded in orgasm.

The three of us slid to the ground in a tangle of naked limbs and lay there for several minutes in stunned euphoria. Then, without saying a word, the blonde cop stood, dressed, and returned to her car. She waited while Office McKennzie gave me a passionate kiss. "I'm letting you off easy this time, Casey," she said. "Watch out if I catch you in my speed trap again."

In the light of the blonde's headlights, we both dressed and then drove our separate ways.

Officer McKennzie is still a regular at the club. She shows up every Tuesday like clockwork to watch me dance. And on the drive home I get stopped every time.

But I haven't gotten a ticket yet.

Making Whoopie
by Marilyn Jaye Lewis

Evan's ocean-front home in Maui was a spectacular monument to modernism. Constructed in jutting geometric angles and utilizing windows of a massive height, it created the illusion—at the back of the house, anyway—of a structure having no walls at all. Evan could lie alone in the evening, on the great expanse of his austerely appointed king-sized bed, contemplate the unobstructed panorama of sunset and crashing waves outside his bedroom window— eleven-foot sheets of sheer uninterrupted glass—and feel as if he were the only living soul in God's universe.

The truth, however, was quite different. Evan couldn't remember the last time he'd been completely alone. Not only was Cheng, Evan's cook, in the kitchen directly underneath him preparing dinner, but Evan was currently one of the more famous movie stars in the English-speaking world. Beyond the tall privacy wall that guarded the street-side of his modern edifice of concrete and glass, there was a never-ending parade of people—most of them curious strangers with cameras. Strangers by the thousands, it sometimes seemed to Evan, even in the relative remoteness of Maui. And within the hour, Dorianne and all her luggage would be arriving from Honolulu, en route from Los Angeles. Evan might never be completely alone again.

This was it. This was the final hour. If everything proceeded as planned, Evan and Dorianne would legally be husband and wife before the night was over. It was going to be a small and private ceremony: the bride, the groom and the judge, with Cheng and the judge's wife serving as witnesses. How they had managed to keep the news of the impending marriage out of the papers was still a mystery to Evan, but it was further proof that when he truly desired to keep a thing private, it could be accomplished.

At the age of forty, Evan Crane, who had been in the public eye since his midtwenties, had quite an impressive list of things he had managed to keep private—most notably, a long string of homosexual liaisons.

Dorianne was well aware of most of them, and in fact, had even participated in a three-way with Evan and one of his male lovers once, back in Los Angeles. The result of the tryst had bordered on being disastrous, though. It had started out promising enough. Evan had been impressed, even a little taken aback, by Dorianne's capacity for lust, her willingness to be accommodating with her mouth and to surrender her holes to the repeated poundings of both men. But ultimately, Dorianne had been left sleeping alone in the master bedroom, while Evan and Giovanni had slipped downstairs to fuck without her, like voracious animals, on the living room couch.

"You don't have to deny it, Evan," Dorianne had spat the following morning when Giovanni had left. "You think I couldn't hear you? All that carrying on?"

"Why are you getting so angry?" Evan had shouted. "I warned you Giovanni was insatiable. You knew it was likely to get complicated. I don't even understand why you agreed to do it in the first place."

"Maybe it turned me on to try two men at once, Evan, did you ever consider that? That I might have my own fantasies? Or maybe I did it because I'm trying to understand you better—the things you want. Would that be so horrible, if I cared about you?"

It was at that moment that Evan first realized he might be in love with Dorianne, that she might be 'the one.' She was fiery and not afraid to speak her mind. She didn't kowtow to Evan like everybody else did. He was turned on by her passion, by how she stood her ground, and most of all by how she seemed to genuinely care. Over the years, Evan had learned some hard lessons about how to keep his ego in check and resist the constant temptation to have sex with every woman who threw herself at him. (Or every man, for that matter.) As much as he might have used his fame to score pussy and ass whenever he'd wanted it, he was just as frequently used by the people he'd fucked. They objectified him and never seemed to care who he really was under all that fame as long as they could say they'd fucked him.

Dorianne was not a sycophant; Evan had recognized this from the start. Still, during the first year he'd dated her, there was always another lover hidden somewhere. Perhaps right in Los Angeles, or sometimes a continent away. He went through a whole pack of meaningless sex partners before coming to the obvious conclusion that he could better protect his self-interests by resisting temptation.

Until recently, even Cheng's position as cook had been filled by a much younger man, James, a man whose talents hadn't confined him to the kitchen. Evan stared out at the vivid sunset and thought about James. What a little slice of heaven he'd been in the beginning, before he'd gotten envious of Dorianne, before he'd gotten contentious and belligerent, acting more like a spurned lover than as an employee, then Evan had been forced to let him go. Evan felt his cock twitching beneath his linen trousers at the mere thought of James, though. Not that James had been a better lover than Dorianne, but he had been incredibly convenient. James had never seemed to aspire to anything higher in life than to suck or be fucked. Evan could summon James day or night and be obliged with a blowjob on the spot. James seemed happy to be on his knees—on the kitchen tiles, on the bathroom marble, or out on the concrete lanai in the moonlight, as the furious waves crashed against the black lava rocks beneath them. James had an eager mouth and he swallowed without flinching. His devotion to servitude made him irresistible in any position. It hadn't been unusual for Evan to disturb James in the middle of the night, to wake him from a sound sleep, and James would never complain. He'd obligingly turn over and pull down the blankets. He was always naked under those blankets, Evan remembered; always ready. And he didn't require any of that delaying foreplay as long as Evan was sufficiently lubed.

Evan's hardening cock began to ache with the visceral memory of how effortless and uncomplicated it had been to fuck James. James would part his legs, raise his rump slightly and let Evan mount him. His asshole always seemed responsive, too; relaxed—ready for Evan's substantial tool as it ploughed into him. James never protested. He'd lay quietly on his stomach and whimper a little, but give Evan complete access to that tight, hot passageway until Evan's cock had had its fill of fucking it.

He glanced at the bedside clock now; trying to gauge if he had enough time to jerk-off before Dorianne arrived from Honolulu. Evan loved thinking about fucking James' ass and jerking-off. It wasn't that Dorianne didn't turn him on, or that she refused to take it up the ass, in fact when she was in the right mood, Dorianne could get just as filthy and take it just as hard as any man Evan had ever fucked. But getting her in the right mood for anal sex was sometimes a chore, she was a little intimidated by it. Evan was almost *too* endowed; his equipment, he knew, was huge. It was part of why he'd lasted so long in Hollywood.

Assuming she arrived on time, Evan figured he had just over forty-five minutes to get where he wanted to go. That was plenty of time. He pulled open the nightstand drawer for a squirt of his favorite lube and the one, lone filmy stocking Dorianne had left behind last time caught his eye. She was definitely worth her weight in gold, that woman. She had such a nasty imagination.

Evan retrieved the stocking from the drawer and studied it, remembering how she had tormented him, using the stocking to tie his hands behind him then bending him over the bamboo trunk at the foot of the bed. She'd alternated licking his balls that night with an incredibly well-paced rimjob. She had driven his cock crazy by practically ignoring it. Every once in awhile she'd suck the swollen head of his shaft into her mouth, or swipe a dribble of pre-cum from his piss slit with the tip of her tongue, but other than that she'd focused on the rimming. Her delicate hands keeping the taught globes of his ass spread wide so that his puckered hole was at the mercy of her mouth.

Evan knew there'd been no real reason to tie him up for a thing like that, it was something he'd have submitted to willingly, but he liked that she'd pretended he hadn't had any options.

He released his hard cock from inside his trousers, slathered it with the lube and realized James was no longer on his mind. He was wondering instead what it was going to be like to be married. He knew that it was normal for the flame of passion to fade from most marriages, but he couldn't picture it happening between him and Dorianne. Only the night before he'd been half-crazy with lust for her, calling her at her hotel on Waikiki, waking her, insisting they get off together over the phone. Even though she'd been groggy with sleep, he'd known the words that would get to her, trigger her hormones to flow through her like a river of fire, flooding her gorgeous pussy until she was wide awake and touching herself.

"Remember what it was like," his voice had caressed her through the phone wires, "that first time I took you up to my room, back when I had that house in the hills, remember that, Dorianne? What a filthy little girl you were. You really surprised me that night. Remember what I made you do?"

"Yes," Dorianne's breathy voice had come back at him in the darkness. "I remember."

"Tell me what you remember."

"You made me pull up my dress and pull down my panties."

"And what else?"

"You made me get down on my knees."

"And then what did I make you do?"

"Unzip your trousers with my teeth and lick your cock."

Evan loved to hear the word 'cock' coming out of Dorianne's mouth. She had a way of making the whole notion of a cock seem scary to her, scarier than he knew it could possibly be, but it made her mouth sound vulnerable just the same. "That's right," he'd said. "You did such dirty things with my cock that night, didn't you?"

"Yes."

"Why did you do it, Dorianne? Why were you such a nasty little girl?"

"Because," she'd whispered, "I'm your slut, Evan, you know that. I'm a slave to your cock. I'll do whatever you ask me to do as long as I know I can have that big cock of yours in one of my tight holes."

"Oh yeah? Do I get to choose which tight hole I put it in?"

"Yeah."

"Even your asshole, Dorianne? You're going to take me up your tight ass?"

"Yes."

"All the way up?"

"Yes. Even if makes me sweat."

"If what makes you sweat?"

"Feeling myself stretched open back there—your cock is huge."

They had gone on like that for nearly an hour. Evan hadn't been able to stand the idea of hanging up, of being alone without her in his bed, even for the final night. But eventually she'd insisted that she had to get some sleep, even though he hadn't come yet. "I'm going to be a blushing bride tomorrow, Evan, remember? I'm forty-three years old. I'm going to need all the help I can get."

Evan liked the idea that she was older than he was. It satisfied his occasional fantasy of having an older woman take charge of him. "Okay, Dorianne," he'd conceded, preparing to hang up the phone at last, "I'll let you go this time. But after tomorrow, I'm never letting you go again." When they'd each hung up, he'd been alone in the darkness, his fist around his aching cock. Much like he was now—thinking of Dorianne naked, her long legs parted, revealing the closely-clipped black hairs that set-off the fiery pink flesh of her engorged pussy when she was fully aroused, breathing hard and waiting for him to mount her.

Evan loved the sight of her like that. He knew from experience that she would cry out and clutch at his hair, his back, his ass, when he finally laid down on her, penetrated her and gave it to her hard.

He liked to hear her passionate cries in his ear. Sometimes it sounded as if she were in pain.

His fist slid languorously over the slippery head of his cock as he thought about Dorianne and those cries she made. In his mind, he replayed the night he and Giovanni had both gone at her—it was one of his favorite memories. She'd gotten especially worked up when she was on all fours getting it at both ends at once. Giovanni had had a firm grip on her ass as he'd pounded his uncut meat into Dorianne's vagina. Evan's eyes couldn't get enough of watching it. He'd been on his knees in front of her, his erection filling her mouth as she grunted from the force of Giovanni's rhythm. Evan had dug his fingers into Dorianne's hair, grabbing it in fistfuls while he'd fucked her mouth hard. He'd known they were getting rough with her, but she seemed to be wildly into it.

Evan worked his cock more vigorously now, tugging it faster, in time to the visions replaying in his head. He loved to think of Dorianne as a slut, as his own perfect slut, taking whatever he could dole out. He couldn't wait to be with her again, he hadn't slept with her in nearly a week. Tonight he was going to devour her; he was that ravenous for her sex.

They would be married then, he realized. Somewhere in the back of his brain the thought agitated him—what about the men, he wondered? Was she really going to be okay with his occasional men? She had thought it over. She had said she would deal with it somehow. Bisexuality didn't just disappear because a person uttered some marriage vows. They both knew it.

Evan decided to worry about it later. For now, he wanted to continue watching Dorianne get good and fucked in his head. He knew, for the most part, that she had loved it that night with Giovanni—she had loved being filled up, utilized, put through it for hours. Evan thought about her being on the airplane, flying first class; everything about Dorianne was first class. He figured no one would ever guess—not the flight attendants, the other passengers, or the driver who was waiting for her at the gate. None of them would ever suspect that she was a woman who would prefer to be naked and on all fours, getting it hard at both ends from two men at once.

Mrs. Dorianne Crane.

Evan turned it over in his mind and thought the name suited her perfectly. He wondered if she was going to keep her own name—he'd never bothered to ask. He'd try to remember to ask her later. He was concentrating now on having her to himself, having her naked and underneath him; his swollen cock pushing into her vagina and feeling it open for him. He was so tired of fucking his own hand. He wanted to feel his chest pressed down against her soft breasts, her legs wrapped around him tight, her hands grabbing onto his ass and holding him down, grinding against him, like she couldn't get enough of his hard cock in her hole...

He was very close to coming; he could feel the pressure in his balls when he heard her downstairs. Damn, she was either early or he'd miscalculated.

He swung out of bed, hurried into the bathroom to wash his hands, wipe off his cock and zip it neatly into his trousers. It was probably better this way, he thought. Tonight his orgasm would explode into her and she would be in his arms.

Evan headed down the stairs and could see Dorianne in the kitchen, talking animatedly with Cheng. She was smiling; she was beautiful. She's definitely first class, he told himself again. Evan hoped it would last a lifetime. He was going to give it his best shot.

Nobody's Business
by Craig T. Vaughn

I gotta admit it. I have this thing for ass-fucking. Am I a pervert? Maybe. But I don't care. If it works for me and my lover than it's nobody else's business, right? Don't ask, don't tell—you know what I'm saying? The truth is, I like every part of the equation, from checking out a pair of well-packed jeans, to revealing the naked haunches of a new lover, to slip-sliding my tool inside that tightest of entryways. I collect experiences, returning to my favorites over and over again in my mind. These images are better than fantasies, because they're real.

The summer after graduating college, I had an "ass fling" with a beautiful girl. From the first time I laid eyes on her, I knew we were going to fuck, to do it the way I like—hard and raw, skin connecting with skin. Charlene Miller was twenty-four, built slender but with corded muscles. Her golden hair fell forward over a sunkissed face. Light played tricks in her eyes, turning them grey one instant and pure silver the next. She shined, no question about it. She had an innocent quality that drew people to her.

And she had an ass that made me dizzy.

Whenever she wore her tight, faded jeans, I would lose myself in instant daydreams starring her tied down to my bed and me wielding my mammoth hard-on. I wanted to fuck her, but I also wanted to watch her being fucked, to see her face grow flushed, her eyes shut tight with the confusion a pleasure that decadent would bring. I had visions of slipping off her well-worn Levis, of oiling up her asshole with my spit and ravaging her from behind.

Charlene worked in a Beverly Hills office building that housed movie studios, a modeling agency, and the record company that produces my band. She served coffee and sweets in the downstairs café. All of the men in the offices went crazy for her, but Charlene paid no particular attention to any one of them. This added to her appeal. Because she didn't care, the guys flirted outrageously as they slipped extra dollar tips into the blue jar by the cash register. They stretched out her name, "Charrr-lie," smiling as they said it. You could picture them in her bed, saying it. You could visualize them in the back of her red convertible Cadillac, sighing as her hungry mouth got busy between their legs. "Oh, Charlene, yessss."

But I won. I've relaxed in the back seat of Charlene's car. I've smiled as I've said her name the morning after. I've stroked that glossy hair away from her forehead. I've been the boy in the bed.

You might not put us together naturally. I'm all Hollywood rock and roll. Tall, tattooed, and thin, with dark hair and shadowy eyes. I wear a standard uniform of black jeans and black T-shirts every day of the year, and I pull my long hair off my face into a ponytail unless I'm playing. Then I let it loose and wild, to whip around me as I move. And while Charlene's skin is bronzed from healthy weekends spent outdoors, I'm as pale as they come from long days spent in cave-like clubs rehearsing and performing. Yet we fit together, fit like pieces in a fantasy puzzle, my cock buried to the hilt in her perfect ass, shame coloring her cheeks an electric rose.

Every single time I went into the café, I sent her silent messages with my eyes. I'd buy a nectarine from the basket on the counter, and while she rang it up, I'd think about squeezing the ripe fruit in my hands until it dripped sticky sap on her body. My eyes flickered with images of lubing her asshole with the flesh from a melon, of pulling down my jeans and fucking her. Just fucking her.

Of course, I've been fucked this way, myself. I'm not one to dish out what I can't take. My introduction to the world of anal delights is clear in my memory. Not only do I possess a mental movie of that night, I remember the soundtrack, the words spoken, as well. My college girlfriend liked to talk while we fucked. Whenever we messed around, Veronica kept up a running monologue, telling me what she was going to do a split second ahead of time. She liked me because I'm the strong, silent type. I let her ramble, got into the melody of it, grooved on the sound of her voice.

On the night of my first ass-fucking, she asked for permission first. "Really?" I said. "You'd like that?" Yeah, I knew she was edgier than most of the co-eds, but this managed to surprise even me.

She was alive with nervous energy, moving too quickly around the room, gathering her toys, her implements, promising me that I'd love every minute. Curiosity piqued, I let her bend me over the green comforter on her bed, and I waited as she got her strap-on cock wet with spit. Then she pressed her lips to my ear and hissed, "Kelly, I'm gonna take your back door."

Honestly, I wasn't sure how to feel about this. Did it make me a girly-boy? Some sort of a fag? But deep down, I wanted to know what it would be like. And Veronica understood this. She wrapped her arms around me and slid the head of her cock between my asscheeks. As she pressed forward slowly, she said, "Relax, baby, let me in." I took a deep breath, feeling the bulging head of her cock pushing forward, and I clenched. I couldn't help it. My entire body tensed so tightly I felt as if my muscles were on lock-down.

Veronica knew exactly what to do. She wrapped one fist around my cock and pumped up and down. Then she started in with what she did best: talking. Her voice was soothing. "This turns you on so much, Kelly, just the thought of it. Look at how hard your cock is. Now you've gotta open up for me."

But my body would not obey. For a moment, Veronica didn't move. The head of her plastic cock and the first inch of the shaft were between my asscheeks, but she remained entirely still. Then, slowly, she began to rub back and forth, not pushing toward my entrance, but sort of tickling me with her toy. I liked that feeling, and I sighed and then moaned. At my response, she picked up the pace, pushing more of the shaft between my cheeks, still working my cock with her magic hand.

She said, "You're rock-hard, Kelly. You don't know what you want. Your brain might think it's wrong, but your body's screaming for it to happen." To prove her point, she took one of my own hands and put it between my legs, and I took over for her, working myself fiercely, feeling my climax rise. As I played, I stopped being concerned with what it all meant and started concentrating on coming.

Veronica said, "It's good being filled, isn't it, Kelly..." and then her voice trailed off. I wasn't used to a time when my girlfriend didn't talk. She always had to tell me how good it felt or how sweet I tasted. Now, she was speechless, her faux cock pushing toward my asshole again. Then she said real quiet, "*You* talk, Kelly. Tell me how it feels. Please—" Her voice was hoarse.

I took a deep breath, then started. "It hurts good." As I spoke, my body relaxed and let her in. "Does that make sense?"

"Sure it does, baby. Sure it does. Keep talking." Carefully, she pushed forward. The muscles of my ass squeezed her, giving her a welcoming embrace. "What are you thinking, Kelly?" she asked next. "Paint a picture for me."

I closed my eyes. I wasn't sure at first *what* I was feeling. But then, in my head, I suddenly saw the act in reverse. I started describing my fantasy to Veronica. "That's my cock you're riding," I told her through gritted teeth, "I'm fucking you." I dug my body back into hers, ramming her cock all the way into me. "It feels good, doesn't it, Veronica? Being fucked like this..."

Her body was frozen.

I was doing all the work, bouncing on her cock, keeping her inside me, connecting me to her so that it was difficult to tell where one of us ended and the other began. "Can you feel me inside you?" I asked her. "Can you feel my cock in your ass?"

It was an illuminating moment for me, seeing this different view, and I came from the image, slowing my rocking motion on her pole, shooting all over the bed. She followed quickly, shuddering as she climaxed, then staying joined to me for a long time. And even after she'd pulled out, we held each other, our bodies entwined on the sofa, neither one of us saying a word.

That was my introduction to the beauty of back-door romping, and it was the beginning of a new era in sexual variations for me. And with this new era came new power. I started to look for girlfriends who would like what I liked. I would get a sense about them, a feel for the type of energy they gave off. It got so I could go into a club and spot the chicklet I would take home.

And then I saw Charlene. She wasn't an easy mark because she didn't know she wanted what I had to give. But once I decided on her, I turned my attention toward the pursuit. I visited the café more often than usual, on days when I didn't even have a meeting with my producer. I sat at a table with a book, and I surreptitiously stared at the blonde-haired angel behind the counter.

It took about a week before she smiled back at me, almost a month before she began slipping me notes when she handed me a cup of coffee, little sticky Post-its on my cups that said: "You make my panties wet when you look at me like that." And a month after that, we were meeting near the loading docks on her breaks, pressing each other up against the stucco wall of the building.

I worked slowly. I didn't want to scare her off. I have a pretty good sense for people, and I got the feeling that she'd never been taken the way I wanted to take her, that she'd never been pinned down on a bed and fucked from behind. I wanted to seduce her, to plant the idea in her head and make it her fantasy. And then make her fantasy come true.

During our midday meetings, I stroked her pussy through her ripped-up jeans. I French-kissed her, leaning my body against hers, devouring her mouth, drinking in her scent. I made her come inside of her 501s, the crotch all drippy wet with nectar. I made her look into my eyes and say, "What're you doing to me, Kelly?" her lips curving into an embarrassed grin, "You're driving me crazy, you know it?"

I planned on driving her crazier still.

"I want you here," I said, reaching my hands around to cup her sweet asscheeks in her jeans. "I want to fuck you there—"

She tilted her head up to look at me, but she didn't speak.

"You want that, too, don't you, baby?

And she nodded. It was all the encouragement I needed.

When I first took her ass, it happened on top of a desk in my producer's office. He gave me the key, and then disappeared, as I'd requested. As planned, Charlene met me after she got off of work. I locked the door and stripped off my jeans. Charlene stared as I slid my boxers off, then sat down on the edge of my desk. I took her hand and put it around my cock. I let her feel it and then I put my hands on the back of her neck and pushed down so that she bent close to my tool.

She parted her lips and took the head of my cock into her mouth as I ran my fingers through her hair. "That's it," I whispered, "that's right, get it nice and wet for me. You know where it's going."

I wanted her to feel the way *I* had my first time. I wanted it to be an eye-opening experience. I let her suckle me, get the head of my cock and then the shaft lubricated with her spit. Then I pushed her back and ran my fingers up and down my cock, stroking it, rough-handling it. Charlene took a step back, watching me. She had her hands on the buckle of her belt, but she hesitated. I knew what she needed, and I gave it to her.

"Take your pants down, Charlie," I said. "You don't have to take them all the way off, just take them down to your knees."

She'd never moved so quickly before.

"Now, bend over the desk." I stood and watched as she bent over, gripping into the side of the wood with both hands. She trembled, and then ducked her head. She wouldn't meet my eyes. I moved behind her, rested my cock against her naked ass, and brought my arms around her.

"Feel that?" I asked softly, "Feel it pressing against you?"

She nodded.

"I'm going to put the whole thing inside you," I said, never raising my tone. "It's gonna slide right inside your tight, virgin asshole and it's gonna feel so good it will seem unreal."

She shuddered again, then looked over her shoulder at me. I was glad we were here, in a neutral zone. If we'd been at my place, I would have wanted to tie her down. But this was better, watching her hold herself as still as she could. This was much more my speed.

"It's okay, Charlie," I told her, "we'll go nice and slow."

She seemed to relax when I said that, so I took it as the opportune time to get out my lube, slick up my rod, and slide it between her dimpled asscheeks. She sucked in her breath, then let it out in a rush. I didn't enter her, just pressed against her asshole, rocking back and forth to let her get used to the feeling. I dropped one hand in front of her and began to play with her dripping pussy, getting her nice and wet there.

When I felt the first contractions of her cunt, I drove the head of my rod into her ass. She jumped at the intrusion, then settled himself, her arms gone rigid and her knuckles white. I said, "You do it, Charlie. You work yourself back on me, taking it in at your own pace." I didn't stop tugging at her clit, but I let her decide how she wanted to play.

I could tell that she didn't think she could do it. My fucking her was one thing, but her fucking herself with my cock was something else entirely. But finally, and slowly, she pushed back on me. She took a bit more of the shaft inside, adjusted to it, and pushed again. She moaned and pressed back more, getting daring, taking it in to the hilt and then rocking on it. Then she said, "Now *you*. I can handle it now, you do it."

Music to my ears. I gripped into her shoulders and started what I do best, fucking her rhythmically. Not too hard or too fast, but just hard and fast enough. I talked softly to her while my hips slid forward until our bodies were pressed together. I said, "That's it, that's the girl, you touch yourself," and I felt the muscles in her right arm jerk to life as she began stroking her clit.

I learned from the way she moved, and began working to the beat she needed, matching her thrust for stroke. Her fingers went in and out of her cunt and my cock went in and out of her rear door. I never let the head slip out, but the shaft did the trick, stimulating places she'd never known about, building in both speed and intensity when I could tell she was about to come.

She climaxed before she knew what was happening. Lost in a double world, her hand bringing her the normal pleasure that she was well-used to, my cock fulfilling her darkest, unspoken dreams.

I held her, still inside her, and then slowly pulled out. She was flustered, couldn't figure out what to do next. When she turned around, I put my hand under her chin and made her lift her gaze to mine. I said, "Don't be embarrassed, Charlie. I wanted to do that from the moment I met you."

That made her grin, and confess to me something I would never have guessed. She said, "I've wanted that, too, Kelly, I wanted that, too."

Everyone has a plan. Everyone has an agenda. I was so busy with mine that I never stopped to consider the fact that she might have one of her own.

On Fire
by Sarah Clark

I'm in love with a firefighter. She works at the station across the street from my apartment building, and I sit on my fire escape and watch her wash the truck. She's well-built, showing off her biceps in a white tank top, wearing faded jeans that hug her hips and reveal her taut physique. Her muscles are alive beneath her skin, seeming to dance whenever she moves. Sometimes, when she's finished, she stands beneath the spray of the hose after rinsing the truck. I can barely watch that, the revelation of a perfect body in those drenched clothes. The dream turned reality as her jeans get tighter on her thighs and ass. My firefighter has an ass that is what an ass lays awake at night and dreams about being.

When I first took my apartment, the landlady warned me about the location. She said, "You'll hear sirens all the time. Night and day. Will that bother you?" The window was open and I went to it and looked out.

The previous tenants had left the window box filled with pale pink baby roses. I drank in their heady fragrance as I looked at the station below. My first vision of my firefighter was petal-scented. I saw the bright red truck. I saw the magnolia tree in blossom on the corner. And I saw her. Five or six other firefighters moved around the gleaming truck, but I couldn't tell you what they looked like. They were merely bit-players, while she was the star of my fantasies.

My firefighter has golden skin and blue eyes. Her black hair is straight and glossy. She usually keeps it short, but now it's getting a little bit long in the front. She has to push it out of her eyes sometimes when she works. I imagine doing the job for her, running my fingers through that midnight hair, staring into her sky blue eyes before bringing my mouth to hers. She has full lips—lips to be licked, to be bitten at the tail end of a long, steamy French kiss.

"Will the sirens be a problem?" the landlady asked again, moving closer to me and speaking slightly louder as if I were hard of hearing.

I shook my head "No," then explained that I'm an insomniac. I work nights at a 24-hour café, serving coffee and breakfast to truckers at 2 a.m. I drink enough java myself that I stay up half the day, only crashing for a few hours in the middle of the afternoon.

Mornings, I reserve for watching her. I slip out of my starched pink uniform with the white piping, change into cut-offs and a T-shirt, slick back my short blonde hair, then wait for her to appear outside. Wait for her to look up and see me. She's not there everyday, but I sit and wait anyway, rolling movies in my mind from previous visions of her, images that I now own.

I've choreographed what it would be like to meet her. In some versions, I call out, offering her a cool glass of lemonade, bringing it downstairs and across the street. Often, in these fantasies, I'm naked beneath my short white robe, and I let the neck of the robe slip open as I hand her the glass. She takes the lemonade from me, then fishes out an ice cube and runs it, sticky and sweet, along my collarbones, down the flat line between my ribs. The cube grows smaller as it makes its way along the shallow of my belly.

I have a tattoo of a butterfly just below the indent of my waist. I know that she would trace the ice along the outline of my butterfly's wings, that my tattoo would glisten under the shimmering coating and seem to come to life.

We've had a long, hot summer, and I easily visualize the ice cube melting on its way to meet my pussy, trailing translucent lemon-scented water down my body. I can picture my firefighter on her knees on the blazing hot cement, parting my nether lips and thrusting the chip of ice deep inside me, then sealing her mouth to my honeypot and sucking the drops of moisture as they drip free.

I find myself with one hand on the seam of my frayed denim shorts as I watch her. Unaware of my own actions, I place my palm against the split of my body, cupping myself and rocking back and forth on this fulcrum. Wanting *more*, as I watch her muscles shift and glide with the effort of her work. Wanting her to lift me up on that engine, bind me to one of the ladders, hose me down with a spray of water.

At the diner, during the four a.m. slump when I have only two or three customers in my section, I find myself thinking about her. I wonder where she goes when she's not at the station. I've caught glimpses. I saw her biking along the beach early one Sunday morning when I was walking home from work. I'd stopped on the walkway that follows the Palisades to look at the houses below, the millionaire homes that face the water. They have hidden gardens behind tall fences, but you can see inside when you're on the cliffs.

My firefighter was biking along the path, her head down, dark hair falling over tanned forehead, legs pumping piston-fast as she headed toward Venice. I wished I had my bike to follow her, wished I was down below with her, rather than observing, as always, from above.

I fantasized about standing at the side of the bike path, of her looking up and seeing me, stopping, getting off her bike. I could picture her taking my hand and walking with me in the sand, toward the sea. Neither of us caring about the lacy edge of foam licking up at our feet. Walking further into the water, drenching our clothes, meeting and melting in an embrace as the silver waves washed in around us.

My fantasies easily change, like dreams, and in the water our clothes are suddenly gone. She moves forward, pressing into me, her lips on the hollow of my throat, her kisses burning hot, setting me ablaze while the cool waves lap at our skin. I know the taste of her lips, salty from the ocean breeze, sweet because they're hers. I know the feel of her body as it presses against me. I know that when she grips my arms and stares into my green eyes she feels the same thing that I do: Complete. Wanted.

After months, I learn her name. One of the other firemen calls out to her, "Hey, Kendra...." And now, I have something further to use in my fantasies, a new ingredient to stir things up.

I whisper her name as my fingers find their secret place in between my legs and make those magic, mystic circles. My head back on my pillows, my slender hips arched forward toward a dream lover, I say her name aloud, "Kendra, please..." feeling her hands on me, stroking my body, starting a bonfire within me by keeping me on edge. She doesn't give me what I want, not at first. She teases me, holding her body well above mine, taunting me with her lips instead, giving me long, luscious kisses. My mouth is open, hungry. I feel her breath, feel her lips on mine. She props herself up, using those fine muscles in her arms, not letting skin touch skin.

It's hot outside. It's hotter in my bed.

"Please, Kendra..." my voice is louder now, but I don't care. It's mid-morning, the rest of my neighbors have gone to work. I'm ready for sleep, and this is one of the ways I know to bring it. Climaxing and sliding into a dream world, in which Kendra is featured as my one true love. But I can't come, regardless of my knowledgeable fingers, of my chanting her name. I stand, wrap my silk robe around my body, and make my way to the fire escape.

She's below, washing the truck with three other firefighters. Her hair is off her face, her body is hard and lean in faded jeans and a tank. Her buddy pokes her and she suddenly looks up at me. I feel the heat of her eyes on mine. I run my fingers through my platinum hair. I start to flush. She calls out, "Where were you? Usually, you're waiting for us..."

My cheeks are crimson. She's seen me. She knows. I practically stutter, starting to say something, but having no idea what. Mid-thought, I change my mind. "Would you like some lemonade?"

She grins at me. It drives me wild, changes her face from one of mastery and art, the lines and bones of her features shifting into a vision of tomboyish charm. Her buddy nudges her again, nodding, eyes wide, saying, "Go on... go on..." Can't hear her, but I get the meaning. Kendra sets down the soapy sponge, wipes her hands on her thighs, waits for a break in traffic, and crosses the street. She looks up at me. I forget what I'm supposed to do, until she says, "Are you going to buzz me in?"

I nod, rush inside, hit the buzzer, then open the door and stand on the landing. She takes the stairs two at a time. She must, because she's in front of me in seconds. Then, shyly, she just stands there and looks down at me. For the first time, she is above, she is in charge. I wait. she waits.

I say, "My name's Elena."

"Kendra."

"I know."

She smiles. We continue to stand in the hallway. I feel hot, too hot. My face is flaming, my heart beating too fast. She says, "You mentioned lemonade..." and I nod and lead her into my apartment. I walk into the kitchen, my bare feet padding on the white and black tile floor. She strides past me to the living room and lowers the blinds on the window. "Don't need my friends keeping an eye on me."

I blush harder as I bring her a glass of lemonade. Chips of ice bob in the pale liquid. She takes the glass from my hand, sips from it, looks me over.

"I've seen you up there, on your escape," she says.

"I didn't know. You never look at me."

"I'm sly, I guess, didn't want to stare."

She's staring now, at the opening of my robe, at the place where silk meets skin. I am so hot. I need her to cool me down. Could I say it? Could I simply describe my fantasies and let her make them real? She's a firefighter. She'd know what to do.

She says, "I've got to tell you something," then pauses as if she's not sure if she can get up the nerve.

"Please..." I say.

In a rush, "I fantasize about you all the time, Elena."

I swallow hard.

"I mean, you're so pretty, sitting up there. I've pictured you on our truck, letting me wash you with the sponge, the soapy water all over your body, rinsing you off with the soft spray, making your skin gleam in the light."

I can't take my eyes off her. She puts one hand under my chin and strokes the line of my neck with her thumb. She searches out my pulse point, the aching beat of blood through veins, and she stops talking, mesmerized by my inner rhythm.

"I've thought about you, too...."

And I tell her. I confess. About the ice, about the thrill of it on my skin, still speaking as she leads me to the bedroom, as she tilts the glass and takes a piece of ice between her lips, as she presses this frozen heaven to my cheekbones, my own lips, the hollow of my neck. Moving lower, opening my robe carefully, sliding it free from my shoulders. Numbing my nipples, first one, then the other, then pinching the cold flesh as she moves the ice in a line down my belly, getting nearer, nearer.

The chip is gone before she reaches my delta of Venus. She spreads me out on the bed and brings the lemonade with her, taking another piece of ice between her lips and tracing it between my breasts, down my belly, to the fluttering wings of my butterfly tattoo. The ice is gone again, but she doesn't get another piece. She uses the tip of her tongue to trace my butterfly's vibrantly colored wings. She goes around and around with her tongue on my skin, and I'm spiraling downward with each flickering touch.

She looks up at me, up the line of my body, her mouth curving into a grin, and then she takes another sip of lemonade and sets the glass on my nightstand. I look at it instead of her as she moves between the split of my legs and presses her icy mouth to the outer lips of my pussy. Then the chip of ice is suddenly thrust forward and her mouth is sealed to me, drinking me in, drinking each drop of my come as it pools inside me, and finally I look at her and into her luminous eyes.

She says, "Elena," as if she's naming me, claiming me. I moan. Can't help it. The movies in my mind are playing at fast-motion, letting me see each frame a second before she makes fantasy come true.

"We'll go slow later. We'll go slow after..."

And I nod, understanding, needing it as hot and fast as she does. I've wanted this way too long.

She says, "I have to be inside you."

"Yesssss...." I say, thinking, oh, God, she's packing.

And her jeans are open and her cock is out and she's above my body teasing me with the head of it before plunging inside me. I'm wet, so wet, and I take her in, grabbing her with the tight muscles of my pussy. She's up on her arms above me, filling me with steady strokes, then moving her hips in small circles that send me reeling with pleasure.

She says, "You're so beautiful. You sit and watch and make me feel ... I don't know..."

"Wanted...." I say... "Complete...."

And she swallows hard and grabs me to her, turning our bodies so that we're on our sides, and she traces my cheekbones as she rocks inside of me. Her cock is strong and powerful in my body. Her fingers are flames that lick my skin. I'm on fire. I'm burning up.

We kiss as we reach that point together, her rollicking rhythm taking me there, and higher, and there and back, until I'm not thinking anymore, I'm just letting those vibrations wash over me, leaning my head back in the pillow as she opens her eyes and stares into mine.

Her teeth bite into her bottom lip. Her head goes back and her dark hair falls away from her face. She says my name when she comes. She says. "Elena...."

Fantasy turned reality. Movies come to life. Kendra wraps me in her arms. We fade into sleep together to the crackling sound of the ice as it melts in the glass. Our bodies are entwined, our dreams on fire.

Pinch the Head
by Julia Moore

"Pinch the tip, suck the head."

Those were the first words I saw when I got off the plane in New Orleans. The slogan was printed boldly on a vibrant blue T-shirt hanging in the window of an airport souvenir store. I had no idea what the risque statement referred to, but I have to say, my interest was definitely piqued. You never see shirts like that in New York. People are simply too uptight to be caught wearing them. That was one of the reasons why I'd wanted to go to New Orleans. Although it's difficult to believe a city like Manhattan could ever be boring, I was a girl who needed a change of scenery.

"But Kate, you know what conventions are like," my friend Janice had said, surprised that I'd volunteered for floor duty at the trade show.

"It's *The Big Easy*," I'd countered, having heard all about the festive atmosphere.

"You won't even make it to Bourbon Street," Janice had predicted. "By the end of the day, you'll crash in the hotel with room service and bad TV movies."

I took my chances, and I packed my sexiest dresses as well as my normal business suits, planning on mixing plenty of pleasure with my business. Since Todd moved out four months ago, my sexual cupboards had been bare. Unfortunately, after two mind-numbing days trapped in the convention center, I decided that was Janice was right. This trade show was like all others: Smiling until your face hurt, pretending that you were happy to see every geek who walked by.

That's when I spotted him—a man who was obviously not part of our group. Unlike the rest of the suit-clad drones, he looked rebellious in Levis and cowboy boots. Tall, with short dark hair and a wicked smile, he instantly captured my attention. When I passed him in the hall, I couldn't help but notice his deep green eyes, and the fact that those eyes were focused on me. His gaze made me feel as if being naked with him would be a very good thing.

That night, as I looked out of the hotel window toward the French Quarter, I imagined slipping on my slinkiest black dress and searching for my mystery man. I wondered whether he would be able to live up to his bedroom expression. I also wondered if maybe he could explain those intriguing slogans to me. Not only "Pinch the Tip..." but one I'd seen on another T-shirt: "Shuck Me, Suck Me, Eat Me Raw."

Or perhaps he could demonstrate the actions for me.

Staring into the night, I lifted my nightgown and slid one hand into my panties, fantasizing about making love to this dark stranger while passengers on dinner cruises watched us from the Mississippi. But even though I rubbed my swollen clit until I thought it would burst from the friction, I still went to bed unfulfilled. I am a strong believer in self-satisfaction, but every now and then a girl needs to ride a real live cock.

The next day, I wore a cherry red silk dress with buttons running the length in the front. I paired it with crimson high heels and put my dark hair in an upsweep that gave me a hint of a bedroom air. Just as I'd hoped, I ran into my handsome stranger everywhere. When I emerged from one early morning conference, I found him leaning by the coffee stand. At lunch in the cafeteria, he was at the counter when I made my purchase. Yet, despite our sizzling eye contact, neither one of us spoke.

Finally, I skipped a 3:30 lecture to look for him. My time in New Orleans was drawing to a close. I needed to act if I wanted any excitement at all. Luckily, it didn't take me long to locate him in the café, talking to the bartender. He smiled and nodded to a booth in the corner, as if he'd been expecting me, and when he walked over, he held a beer in each hand.

"Isn't it a little early?" I asked, looking over the bottles of Voodoo

Lager. The labels were adorned with an image of a swamp.

"I'm off for the day," he said, speaking in a sensuous New Orleans drawl. I took a sip of the dark beer and tried to think of something else to say so that I could hear him speak again.

"So you work here?" Brilliant conversational gambit, but every time I met his gaze, I had visions of being undressed with him on the banks of the Mississippi. This made it difficult for me to speak coherently.

"In charge of concessions," he told me, instantly explaining why I'd always seen him near the food court or coffee counters.

"Now, you're finished—?" I let the question hang to see if he'd introduce himself. He got the hint. Reading my name tag he said, "Kate, my name's Mike, and I was wondering if you'd like a tour."

"Of the city?" I asked, excited.

"No, the center."

"I've been stuck inside here for days," I said, thinking about my nighttime fantasy of making love to him on the river's edge. How was I going to work *that* into the conversation? My mind raced, and then I took a chance. Leaning forward, I whispered the question that had been in my head since first arriving in New Orleans.

"Pinch the tip, suck the head," I murmured. "What in the world does that mean?"

Mike burst out laughing. Then he repeated the words, pronouncing 'head' like 'haid,' before explaining. "That's how you eat a crawfish. You know, those little red creatures that look like miniature lobsters.

I felt myself flush, but that didn't stop me from continuing my query for knowledge. "And 'Shuck me, suck me, eat me raw—'"

Maybe there was something in the way I said it, because Mike's cheeks reddened, too. "It's the proper way to eat an oyster," he said softly.

After that, we just stared at each other for a minute. I was thinking about how much I wished I were an oyster, and I'm sure Mike was having his first feelings of jealousy toward a crawfish.

"About that tour, Kate," Mike said, his voice gone husky, "you haven't seen the center from an insider's perspective."

I understood now that he was talking about more than your average lookaround, and I nodded. Quickly, Mike led me from the cafeteria and up a series of stairs to the top of the center. Electricity flickered between us, just from the touch of his hand in mine. There was a magnetic energy between the two of us, urgent and undeniable.

At the top landing, Mike pulled out a ring of keys and opened an unmarked door, asking, "Ever been on a catwalk?" I shook my head and followed him onto the walkway. Here, we looked down on the main floor of the convention center, covered with booths. For a moment, I became so mesmerized I almost forgot that Mike was standing next to me. That is, until I felt his firm body pressed against mine.

"Can they see us?" I asked as he wrapped his strong arms around me.

"If they looked up."

I had worked for almost three days on the floor without looking up once. Now, I stared at our reps leading customers through the sales pitch and felt extraordinarily happy not to be there with them.

"Why are you smiling?" Mike asked. Rather than explain, I turned around and kissed him. He seemed to expect it, because he brought his arms around me and pulled me close, kissing me back in a way that told me he knew what he was doing. His tongue was warm in my mouth and it made spiraling designs that had me dizzy with pleasure. I followed his lead, my heart racing as he brought his hands up my body, stroking me through my dress as he continued to kiss me. When his fingertips brushed my nipples, they stood out hard, ready for more. Ready for him to kiss them, to lick and bite them.

As if he'd read my mind, Mike unbuttoned the front of my dress and softly stroked my breasts through my black lace bra. Then, moving faster now, he unfastened the clasp and released my twin globes. My breasts are small and round, with nipples a deep rose-colored hue. Mike silently admired them for a moment, before leaning forward. I thought I would faint when he brought his mouth to them, sucking on my right nipple then my left, then nipping them between his teeth, exactly as I had fantasized about only moments before. Then he licked in a line back up my chest to my throat, pressing his lips to my pulse point as if wanting to feel my heart beating. As he worked, I felt Mike's erection against me, and suddenly I couldn't wait any longer.

I took a step back from him, and he gave me a hungry look, as if he didn't want to be interrupted from his kissing games.

"Let me," I said, unable to formulate any other request. Mike seemed to understand, because he waited patiently as I bent on my knees on the catwalk and unzipped his fly.

There's nothing in this world more exciting to me than meeting a cock for the first time. Each one has a different personality, and Mike's matched his style. Rugged, thick, and finely veined, his prick fit well in my fist as I worked the tip between my lips and into my wet mouth. Mike moaned and gripped the railing for support.

"You're so warm," he whispered, "so warm and soft."

I didn't look down, but I knew about those people on the floor below us, and it made me soak my panties. My skin prickled at the knowledge that my co-workers and competitors were strolling around clueless several hundred feet beneath me. When I stared up at Mike, I saw that he was looking down at them. I could tell that the same thoughts turned him on, too.

Now, I focused my attention on Mike's cock. I licked it from the base to the tip, then ran my tongue all around the head, slowly, as if I were devouring wayward drips from a melting snow-cone. I teased the special area on the underside, the little nerve center that seems to drive most men wild.

In my mind, I remembered the way he'd said to eat a crawfish, and I tried this method on Mike. Pinching the tip very gently, I sucked the head. I know Mike understood what I was doing, because when I tilted my head to look up at him, he shot me a grateful smile. Then I stopped teasing him, and brought the entire length into my mouth until I could feel the tip hammering against the back of my throat. I knew as I sucked him that anyone could see us if they only looked up. This concept made me wetter still, and I slid one hand between my legs and started to work my clit through my panties as I continued to pleasure my new partner. But after only a few minutes of heavy-duty sucking, Mike said, "Stand up, Kate. Please."

Reluctantly, I let his cock slip from my lips and felt his hands on my shoulders, helping me to rise.

"I want you to look at the people down there while I fuck you."

Without hesitating, I took my place at the railing as he got behind me, lifting my red silk dress and sliding my sheer pantyhose down my legs. His plump cockhead, still nice and slick from my mouth, slid easily between my thighs, and he thrust into me several times quickly, as if he needed to learn the feel of my body before slowing down to a steadier pace. While he worked me, he parted the cheeks of my ass to watch his prick go in and out of my pussy.

"You're so beautiful," he said, his voice a low rumble. "I wanted to fuck you as soon as I saw you."

He'd had the same effect on me, and I told him so. Our bodies seemed made for each other. But even better than the way we fit together physically, was the fact that we were sexually in tune. By this I mean, Mike was a talker. I could envision exactly what he was doing, because he moaned and told me how pretty it looked, his throbbing hard-on moving at a steady beat within my cunt. I listened to him, but kept staring down at the people on the floor beneath us. The two visions melted together for me—the people below, and the mental image of what we were doing.

I have to admit that even though it might have meant an arrest, or at the least, the loss of my job, I actually wanted someone to look up and catch us. Seeing the surprise in one of my fellow conventioneer's eyes would have taken me to new heights. Regardless, I was probably lucky that the people below us continued obliviously with their work while Mike's cock did acrobatics inside me.

"You're so tight," he murmured, kissing the back of my neck, then biting the ridge of my shoulder blade and sending shivers through my entire body. "So fucking tight and sweet."

I adore it when a guy talks dirty to me, and I have discovered that the best way to encourage this kind of conversation is to talk back, so I told him what I was thinking. "I wish that blonde girl down there would look up," I said softly. "She'd be able to see your hands on my breasts, your cock going in and out of my pussy." Who knows what she'd have actually been able to see through the glare of the lights, but fantasies have no limits. "She'd wish she were up here instead of me," I murmured.

"Maybe we should invite her to join us," Mike responded, his voice hoarse. Sometimes it gets more difficult to talk as the moment heats up, but I did my best.

"Maybe she'd replace you," I said, moving directly into another one of my long-time fantasies. "You could do the watching while she got on her knees and lapped at my dripping cunt."

"You'd like that?" Mike asked softly. "You'd like it if all I did was watch?"

"I'd like it better if you fucked my asshole while she sucked my clit."

That image did it for him. He groaned and gripped into my waist, slamming his body into mine. Then his hands moved down to my ass and he stretched my cheeks apart and slid his thumb into my asshole, feeling the contractions there as my pussy squeezed his cock. I couldn't keep up the sexy talk either, as his rhythmic pounding created just the sensations I needed. He pushed deep into me as he started to come, and I forced myself to keep my eyes open as I climaxed with him, staring at the people down below us as the orgasm flared through me.

There was a moment of silence while we were still joined together. Then Mike slowly withdrew and adjusted his clothes while I did the same. At least, I did the best I could, but my dress was wrinkled and I could feel that long tendrils of my curls had escaped from my upswept hairdo. No way was I going back to the center. Again, Mike was one beat ahead of me, saying, "Let's use the back exit instead of going through the main lobby."

Once more, I let him take my hand and lead me, and this time I found myself on a different set of stairs than those open to the conventioneers. The main stairs were carpeted in navy with framed artwork on the walls. This stairway was covered in gray linoleum, and the walls were simply whitewashed. "Employees only," Mike explained, shutting the door behind us. "Fewer frills."

For some reason, I found it as exciting to be behind the scenes as it was to be above the convention hall. Mike was a few steps below me when I told him to stop. He looked up at me.

"Do you have time—?" I started, and shot him a sexy look.

"Here?"

I nodded, batting my eyelashes coyly, and while he watched I slipped off my heels and hose and took off my panties. Then I leaned against the handrail. With Mike staring at me, I lifted my dress and spread the lips of my pussy. I gave him a hands-on lesson in how I like to be touched, sliding my middle finger deep inside my still-dripping cunt while I teased my clit with little flicks from my thumb. When I started to moan, my voice echoed in the hallway. This stairwell had amazing acoustics.

Mike shook his head, as if he couldn't believe we were going at it again so quickly, and then got on his knees on the stairs and locked his hands around my waist.

"Hold your lips open for me," he said, and in a second, I felt his warm tongue on my clit, lapping at me from top to bottom. He sensed how much pressure I desired, giving me a few long, slow licks with the flat of his tongue before ringing my clit with his mouth and gently sucking. It was an effort to keep my pussy lips open for him. They grew increasingly slippery as he worked, and it took all my willpower to hold on. I wanted to let go and dig my nails into his back, to grab onto him and pull his face harder against me. Instead, I kept holding on, my long red nails sliding in my juices, my clit growing larger and harder as I got ready to come again.

Before I could climax, Mike released me and stood up. When I gave him what must have been a desperate, begging look, he whispered, "I want you to come on the end of my cock."

That sounded good to me, and I nodded and watched him stand. He had his fly open in no time, and he took me face front for our second round, lifting me up onto the rail and holding me in place while he slipped his cock inside me. I wrapped my legs around his waist as he pressed my body against the wall. We went cruising into it from the start. No subtleties, just his raging hard-on, still slicked up with my pussy juices from our previous encounter, and my cunt, welcoming him with a series of mighty contractions.

"You feel so good around my prick," he murmured in that drawling accent.

Since we were face-to-face, he kissed me, biting my bottom lip hard before moving into a deep, French kiss that left me breathless. I loved the way he teased me, mimicking with his tongue what he was doing down below with his cock, in and out and then swirling around. Then he moved back slightly to whisper, "Which do you like best, Kate? Head or shaft?"

To explain my choices, he slipped in just the plump head of his prick and rocked it against the mouth of my cunt. "Head?" he murmured, before pounding all the way into me and asking, "or shaft?"

I didn't know what to say. I needed them both, needed the way he drove into me, then pulled entirely out and pressed the tip against my clit, stimulating me as he asked again, "Head—" and then drove it home, "or shaft?" It was uncanny. As soon as I craved his full length back inside me, he followed through, fucking me long and slow before teasing my clit all over again.

"Can't you answer, Kate?"

I couldn't. I didn't have an answer. It was all perfect.

"I'll stop if you don't tell me," he warned.

"Both," I told him finally.

"Greedy little thing," he said, continuing with that divine rhythm. Head, then shaft, then head again, bringing me right up to the edge over and over without letting me climax.

Just as I reached the point of no return, I managed to whisper the one nagging question that had been on my mind since we started fucking. "Who uses these stairs?"

He hesitated before answering, looking deep into my eyes. "My boss, for one," he said, and I realized that he felt the way I had up on the catwalk. That it would actually be exciting to be caught, even if it meant the end of his normal routine. Luck was on our side a second time, however, and we made it through our quickie, Mike lifting me easily in his arms as he came deep inside me, without the door on the landing opening.

Afterward, Mike picked up my panties and hose from the stairs and I slid on my shoes and followed him down to the first floor. He pushed open the door and we found ourselves on a brick walkway leading to the river. Evening had come during our last two hours of fucking, and in darkness we walked slowly along the banks. My legs felt weak and the smell of sex lingered on our skin. I wondered what we would do next. Would he thank me and disappear, my handsome stranger staying just that, a convention fling? Would we go to a bar, or to dinner, or head to my hotel room to fuck all night while staring at the lights of the city?

Mike didn't seem to find the silence disturbing. He slipped one arm around my waist while we walked. I started to relax into the moment, not worrying so much about what would happen but focusing on what was happening right now. Like the fact that a river boat filled with dining passengers was making its way down the Mississippi.

"You know, I've never been on one of those," Mike said in his charming accent. "All the years I've lived here."

"Doesn't look too exciting," I said, "just a bunch of tourists floating downstream."

"You'd make it exciting," he countered, stopping to cradle my face in his hands and kiss me. I could taste myself in his kiss, and that sent my heart racing all over again. His cock throbbed against me through his slacks, and Mike pulled back and looked at me. "Seen any other T-shirts you need explaining?" he asked, and I saw a gleam in those green eyes that let me know he was game.

For anything.

Quiet, Quiet
by Lucia Dixon

"Shhh," he said. "Quiet. Quiet—"

"I can't."

"What'd I say?"

"I can't—"

It was his mother's bed. Let's start with that. Sure, we've made love in many bizarre places before, from the board room at his office to the leather table at the salon where I get bi-weekly massages. But this was his mother's bed, and it was in her bedroom, and she wasn't that far away. For my mental comfort, she would have had to be in Guam, or at the very least out at her country club. In reality, she was downstairs on her patio drinking mimosas with her friends, the tinkling sound of her laughter rising up through the open window.

Joshua said, "Just close your eyes, and block out everything else."

How could I? Not only was his mother within hearing range, but her two hundred guests, invited to a sumptuous garden party, were drunkenly milling around the mansion, exploring. And now her youngest son wanted to take me in the middle of the afternoon, in her bedroom, on her expensive white satin sheets.

"Someone will hear us," I hissed.

"Not unless you scream," Joshua assured me. He's never one for false words of comfort. "Now, be quiet and close you eyes, baby, and keep them closed." This time, from his tone of voice, I obeyed. "Hands over your head," he told me next. I did that, too, and felt the familiar bite of cold metal on my skin as he slid a set of handcuffs over my wrists. Like an American Express card, Joshua rarely leaves home without them. He kissed me, and with my lips still parted, he slipped his tie into my mouth and fastened it behind my head. "That should help ease your worries."

I was done for, and I knew it. Gagging me meant that he thought I wouldn't be able to remain quiet on my own.

"Aren't you the slightest bit turned on, Rebecca?" he asked, sounding coy since I obviously couldn't respond. "Aren't you a little bit excited?" The weight on the bed shifted as he stood up. I guessed that he was undressing, and I tensed, listening, first for his mother, and then as I heard him unbuckle his belt and the hiss-soft sound of the leather as he pulled it through the loops. What had I gotten myself into?

"Not answering, Becca?" he asked, teasing. "Then I'll have to find out for myself." He lifted my floral silk party dress, slid my lacy panties aside, and felt the wetness between my legs.

He sighed. "I know my baby, don't I? Now roll over."

This was easier said than done, but I maneuvered myself on the pillows and thickly feathered duvet until I was face down, my wrists slightly twisted in the handcuff chains.

"You might want to put your face in the pillow, sweetheart, 'cause this is going to hurt."

I made some sort of desperate, mewing sound against the gag, and he responded as if he understood, as if he could decode the worried sound of my words, blurred even as they were against the silken gag.

"It has to hurt, Becca. You know that, baby. It *always* has to hurt."

Lowering my head, I reminded myself that I could have avoided the whole mess. Joshua always gives me choices. He'd told me not to wear panties, I'd ignored him, and this was the punishment to fit the crime. If I'd followed his instructions in the first place, he would undoubtedly have chosen a less frightening place to make love, somewhere out in the gargantuan backyard, hidden by a miniature palm tree or lost among the honeysuckle vines. Now, not only were we in his mother's boudoir, he was going to exact his punishment on me with his belt.

"Ten," he said, and I swallowed hard. "Ten here. We'll take care of the rest later."

I wasn't worried about that. In the privacy of our apartment, I can withstand almost anything. Joshua knows this, and because of this fact he rarely lets me get away with being disciplined at home. I didn't have much time to contemplate the future, however, because he was off, striking the first blow with the belt on my naked ass and then lining up the second and third before the first sparks of pain had even properly registered.

As I drew in a gasp, he climbed onto the bed and plunged inside me. His cock sought out the wetness he'd already found with his probing fingers, and it told him everything he needed to know. That despite my protests and attempts to talk him out of the humiliating games he plays with me, I live for them as much as he does.

He struck the fourth and fifth blows while he was fucking me. Pulling back to catch the lowest, roundest part of my ass, and then driving his cock between my thighs, so that the pain was lost against the pleasure of the ride.

"Told you how to dress today, baby. Should have listened to me."

But then, of course, I wouldn't be getting this. The feel of his throbbing cock inside me, perfectly balanced with the pain from the belt.

"When I'm done," he said, coming close to me now that he was whispering, his breath hot against my skin. "When I'm done thrashing you, I'm going to fuck your ass."

My lips started forming begging sounds and I pulled on the chains on my wrists, as if that could possibly help me. The metal made music against the brass railing of the headboard.

"Quiet, baby," he said, "you're the one making all the noise, and I thought you didn't want to be caught."

I tried to obey, hoping that if I were really good for the remainder of the session he might ease up, forget the rest until later. How could he fuck my ass now? When I had to go down and have dinner with his mother and a few hundred of her closest friends. When he knew it would make me cry.

He blocked my worries by continuing with the discipline,

pulling my long hair so that I arched my back, and then slapping my ass in an almost friendly way with the belt. Heating me up with it. I felt the wetness in my cunt spread out to my thighs, and he took advantage of the slippery juices, diving back in me, driving back in me, and then placing the head of his cock on my asshole.

I tensed, and he sensed it, not entering me, but moving away, standing by the bed to finish the job. The belt licked at my skin, and I could picture the blows in my head, the neatness of them, overlapping lines that would be purplish later if I looked at them in the mirror.

He gave me more than ten. He always does. Naming the reasons. How I didn't hold still, didn't behave correctly, didn't accept my punishment like a well-chastised girl should. I never get it right. It's why he loves me.

And then, because he'd told me he would, because he never lies, he climbed back onto the bed and took me, sliding his cock between the cheeks of my ass and then pushing forward, making me grit my teeth, making me grip into the cold metal of the headboard, wrap my fingers around the curlicues of brass, trying to gain some sense of stability when everything in my world was swirling around in weightlessness.

Joshua found a rhythm that went dark and velvety in my head, taking me to far away places with his cock, with the heat that was still in my skin, with the shame that colored my face and made me shut my eyes together even more tightly.

He whispered things to me while he fucked me, told me how pretty I looked captured to the bed. Captured so simply and purely to his mother's bed. The whole fantasy was mixed up, messed up, twisted and dirty, and it made me come, as he must have known it would. Made me come in a series of rapid bucking movements that almost drove him out of me. He held on, though, he's a fighter, kept on going until it was his turn, until he gripped into my arms, bit my shoulder hard through the silky fabric of my dress, and hissed, "Dirty girl. Such a dirty girl. Coming in my mother's bed."

Joshua cradled me afterward, brushed my hair out of my eyes, slid the cuffs off and rubbed the skin on my wrists. He kissed my blushing cheeks and my forehead and the tip of my nose and then whispered to me of how long he'd planned it, how much thought had gone into this tryst. How I couldn't have avoided it if I'd wanted to.

I never can. It's why I love him.

Roger's Fault
by Eric Williams

It was Roger's fault that we were late.

"What a fucking day," he said, looking over at the piles of spreadsheets on my desk. "Let's go grab a beer."

I looked at my watch and shook my head.

"*One* beer," he insisted, and when I told him that I couldn't—when I said that you were at home waiting—he asked, "What are you, man? Pussy-whipped?"

So, Christ, Elena. What was I going to do? One beer turned into two, turned into an hour-and-a-half of playing darts down near the pier at the Rose and Crown. By the time I realized how long we'd been playing, well, it was too fucking late to call and explain, anyway.

"We'll buy her something nice to make her feel better," Roger said, pushing me out the door to the parking lot. I shrugged uselessly. What could that possibly be? Flowers? Candy? No way to buy back nearly two hours of lost time.

"Trust me," Roger said, "I know the perfect gift."

Then we were back in his shiny black pick-up, cruising along Santa Monica Boulevard, through the sumptuous curves of Beverly Hills, cresting into Hollywood. I had my hand on my cell phone, trying to think up some excuse that didn't sound too lame, but he said, "It won't help to call now. We'll just show up with our gift and smooth things over."

Roger acted as if he really knew what he was talking about, and it sounded good, the way he said it. But when he pulled into the parking lot of Tabitha's Toy Chest, I honestly thought he'd lost his mind.

"Come on," I smiled, shaking my head, "I'm not going into a

vibrator store with you." Roger didn't even answer. It was obvious that he'd leave me in the truck if I didn't follow, so I kicked open the door and trailed after him. "You're crazy," I said, but he ignored my words, making me hurry to catch up, tripping down the steps and into the wonderful world of sex toys.

What a sight we made. Two guys in expensive work suits, perusing the aisles of marabou-trimmed nighties, edible panties, inflatable dolls, vibrators, paddles, lubricant. Roger acted casual about the whole thing, as if he shopped in stores like that every day. And then there was me, late as hell already, not knowing what the fuck we were doing there.

"Trust me," Roger said again, this time hefting a huge ribbed purple dildo and poking around in a basket for a suitable leather harness, one that would fit your slim hips without looking foolish. He wanted to find a quality made harness with a delicate buckle. Not too large.

"You've got to be kidding," I said.

"Elena will love it. You'll see."

"You're not buying my girlfriend a dildo."

"You're right," he agreed, and I thought I saw sanity again in my buddy's green eyes. "I'm not buying it. *You* are."

"There's no way."

"Chet," he said, "you can't go home empty-handed. She's going to be upset as a wildcat that you're this late as it is."

"So, what?" I asked him, incredulous. "So I'm going to tell her to strap this thing on and fuck her aggression out on me?"

"Something like that."

And then suddenly, I understood. I'd been set up.

"She told you?" I asked, my voice cracking. I couldn't help but back away from him, standing against what I thought was a wall, but what turned out to be a display of realistic rubber ladies, ready for a man to insert his cock in their mouths, asses, and pussies. Vinyl skin reached out to touch me, and I took a step forward, quickly, then whispered again. "She told you." This time, I wasn't asking.

"No problem with having a fantasy," Roger grinned now. He looked incredibly handsome with that knowing half-smile, his short dark hair, and a start of evening shadow on his strong jaw. "Especially when everyone gets off."

After that, he didn't say anything else. Simply grabbed the items he was looking for, snagged an extra-large bottle of lube from the display by the counter, and paid for his purchases. I have to admit, I had no idea what to do. First, there was the fact of my immediate erection, already making itself known against my leg. I felt as if I were back in high school, getting hard whenever the wind blew— or, more honestly, whenever the little cheerleaders made their way onto the field for afternoon practice. Those tiny pleated skirts flipping up each time they cheered. What filthy mind created outfits like that?

And then there was the fact that my best buddy in the world knew that I wanted my girlfriend to ass-fuck me—and not only me, but to fuck him, as well. It had taken a lot of vodka before I'd confessed that particular kinky fantasy. Never thought the words would make their way to his ears.

Yes, Elena, I should have known, way back when we were sharing secrets. I ought to have guessed that you'd do something like this. Always ready to push the barriers in life, which is why I love you. But thinking back, I realize that's why your blue eyes gleamed so brightly when I whispered the dirty words that made up my most private daydream. In your head, you were already playing this out: Roger and me, on our king-sized bed, and you, the queen of the night, going back and forth between us. Dipping into us. Taking us.

But still, I didn't think it would ever happen.

"Come on, Chet," Roger said, throwing one arm over my shoulder and herding me back to his truck as if he were leading a drunken man to shelter. "Elena's waiting."

At our house, the scene was carefully set. You weren't surprised that we were late, because it was all planned out from the start. The two of you know me too fucking well. Roger was sure he'd be able to coerce me into a game or six of darts. And you knew I'd feel so guilty I wouldn't even have the balls to call. Ten minutes later, back at our house, there we were, Roger leaning hard on the doorbell before I could get my key out, and you, opening the door in your sleek leather pants, tight white tank top, high-heeled boots. You looked so fierce, I could have come on the spot.

"Boys," you said as a greeting. Just that word. Your eyes told me that I should have known better. That I was too slow to figure things out. Before I could respond in my own defense, we were walking after you like bad little kids heading toward the principal's office. Roger was the ring-leader, taking my hand and pulling me down the hall to the bedroom, showing you the present he'd bought and actually undressing you and helping you put it on.

Fuck, Elena, the way you looked stripped down with that harness. Your pale skin, long dark hair, midnight eyes alert and shining. I wanted—well, you know damn well what I wanted. But I'll spell it out anyway. I wanted to go on my knees and get your cock all nice and wet with my mouth, to suck on it until the plastic dripped with my saliva, and then to watch as you fucked my best friend. I wanted to help glide the synthetic prick between the cheeks of his well-muscled ass, to watch you pump him hard, stay sealed into him, then pump in and out again. I couldn't wait to stand against the wall, one hand on my own pulsing cock, jerking, pulling, coming in a shower on the floor. Not caring what kind of mess I made, because, shit, I was beyond caring about anything like that.

That's not what happened, of course. We were in the wrong, coming back late like that. Me, especially, since I had a will of my own. I could have insisted we go back to the house on time. Could have at least called. No, you wouldn't reward me by taking him first, letting me get off easy as the observer. That wasn't your plan.

"Naughty boy," you said. "Roger, help me bend him over."

At your words, there was a tightening in the pit of my stomach, like a fist around my belly. A cold metal taste filled my mouth, and it was suddenly difficult for me to swallow. Roger's seemingly experienced hands unbuckled my belt, pulled off my shoes, slipped my pants off and took down my black satin boxers. Leaving those around my knees, he bent me over the bed, his exploring fingers trailing along the crack of my ass and making me moan involuntarily. Calloused fingertips just brushing my hole. Never felt anything that dirty, that decadent.

He was the one to help you. The assistant. Pouring the oil in a gilded river between my ass cheeks, rubbing it in, his fingertips casually slipping inside of me. Probing and touching in such a personal manner that I could have cried. I wanted him to finger-fuck me, to use two, three, four fingers. I knew what it would be like to have his whole fucking fist inside of me. And, Elena, did I ever want that. Roger, behind me, getting the full motion of his arm into it. But then his strong hands spread me open as you guided the head of that mammoth, obscene purple cock into my asshole. And I wanted that even more.

Jesus fucking Christ, Elena. How did you know? I mean, I told you, of course, that night at the beach, draining the Absolut bottle between us as we stared up at the stars and out at the silver-lipped ocean. Your pussy so wet and slippery as you confessed your secret, five-star fantasy of fucking a guy. And me, harder than steel as I answered that it was what I wanted, as well.

But how did you know how to do it? How to talk like that? Sweet thing like you. Fucking me like a professional and talking like a trucker.

"Such a bad boy, needing to be ass-fucked," you told me, your voice a husky sounding purr. "That's what you need, right, Chet? You need my cock deep in your hole."

That's what I needed, all right, and it was what you gave me. That dildo reaming my asshole, with Roger there, spreading my cheeks wide until it hurt. The right kind of hurt. Pain at being pulled, stretched open. Embarrassment flooding through me and making the pre-cum drip freely from my cock. I could feel the sweat on me, droplets beading on my forehead as I gripped into the pillow and held on. Never been fucked before, never taken, and here my best friend was watching. Helping.

As fantasies go, you never know what will happen when they come true. I turned to look in the mirror on the closet doors as

Roger moved behind you, saw that your bare ass was plenty available since you were wearing only that harness. He wasn't rough with you the way you were with me. He knew how to do it, how you like it. On his knees behind you, parting your luscious cheeks and tickling your velvety hole with his tongue. Playing peek-a-boo games back there, driving the tip of it into your asshole and licking you inside out. Making you moan and tilt your head back, your hair falling away from your face, your cheeks flushed.

Then he was the one to pour oil all over his cock, to rub it in and part your heart-shaped cheeks and take you. I saw a glimpse of his pole before it disappeared into your ass, and the length of it made me suck in my breath. What it must have done to you. Impaling you, possessing you as he took you on a ride.

The three of us fucked in a rhythm together like some deranged beast. You in my asshole and him in yours. Joined and sticky, reduced to animals who simply couldn't get enough. I didn't want to watch, but I had to, as the three of us came, bucking hard in a pile-up on the bed. Groaning, because it was so good. Better than good. It was sublime. Unreal.

But, in my defense, I have to say again that it was all Roger's fault.

Next Friday night, we'll be there on time, Elena. I promise.

Spring Cleaning
by Samantha Mallery

"I've always liked it," Eleanor told me. "I mean, always."

We were seated in the kitchen, sharing a glass of red wine. When Eleanor passed the glass to me, her fingers brushed mine, shocking me with a tiny electric spark. Even though we've been together nearly six years, just the touch of her skin can give me a thrill.

"I don't know," I said, "It doesn't really sound like much of a turn-on to me." I took a sip of the wine and handed it back to her. I enjoy drinking from the same glass she does, lining my lips up with her crimson kiss imprints.

"Just imagine," she started, "you tied down to the bed. Me with a feather duster in my hand, running the pretty pink feathers all over your naked body. You wouldn't be able to stand it."

"That's what I'm afraid of," I told her, honestly. "Not being able to stand it."

Eleanor smiled. "No, this would be in a good way. You'd be squirming, pushing against the bindings, *trying* to beg me to let you go, but laughing too hard to get the words out. I'd tickle you until you came close to wetting the bed."

My eyes must have widened when she said that, because she sensed I was about to agree. "Come on, Jackie," she continued, leaning over the formica kitchen table and grazing my lips with hers in a quick kiss. "You're always up for something interesting."

I thought about it. Interesting, yes. But interesting conjures up images of making love beneath the pier at the Santa Monica Beach, of necking passionately while riding the ferris wheel, of doing it on a train. Tickling didn't fit the concept.

My lover sat back in her chair and regarded me with a look I could not immediately read. Her dark brown eyes seemed thoughtful. She worried her full bottom lip with her teeth, the way she does when she's figuring something out. After a moment she said, "On my next cleaning night, I'll introduce you to the concept. If you don't like it, we can stop. I mean, if you *really* don't like being tickled. But somehow, I think you will."

Eleanor and I take turns planning cleaning nights. The goal is to try and make cleaning our apartment a bit more exciting. It takes the drudgery out of everything from polishing silverware to washing windows. We have come up with sexual uses for even the most mundane household cleaning items, and because we take turns planning, we're always trying to surprise each other. But there's no surprise to the way the evenings end: with our breathing rapid and our bodies shiny with sweat and come. *And* our apartment not much more organized than it was before. Still, scrubbing the shower, or waxing the kitchen floor have both become exciting and hotly anticipated events in our lives because of cleaning nights.

Now, I found myself filled with trepidation at the thought of our next weekend's tickling fest, and wondering how it might be tied in with a cleaning scenario. Would she polish me with a felt rag? Would she tickle me with the scrub brush? Eleanor is a creative woman, I knew she would surprise me.

I am always turned-on, whether I'm in charge of one of these nights, or she is, but this time the fluttering in my stomach was made of something new. Fear? How could I be afraid of being tickled? That just didn't make sense.

On Friday night, I got dressed for our date. I stood for a long time in front of the mirror regarding my reflection. I am five foot six, and I have straight blonde hair that just barely reaches my shoulders. I wasn't sure of the appropriate attire to wear while being tickled. When we have spanking nights (which usually come when we're cleaning the kitchen because of the plentiful wooden spoon paddles), I know to put on a pair of my sweet, lace-edged panties. When we're doing laundry, we'll undoubtedly wind up making love on the washer, and I wear nothing but a terry cloth towel, for padding. But tickling? I ended up in a marabou-trimmed nightgown and robe, with marabou fluff on my high-heeled slippers. The outfit itself practically tickled me when I went to answer the door.

Eleanor nodded her immediate approval. She stood on our patio, a tissue-wrapped bouquet in her lovely hands. I let her in, feeling shy, as I always do when she's in charge. It's fun taking turns this way. It gives us both the opportunity to play different roles. When Eleanor is in charge, her very appearance seems to change. She has light honey-colored hair, and freckled skin. Her eyes are a deep brown, and they seem to glow when she's in charge. They have a heat to them, and they flicker like the purple gold flames in a campfire.

As Eleanor walked into the dining room, she unwrapped the bouquet, and I noticed that it wasn't flowers, but feather dusters, an assortment of four different colors—turquoise, a deep rose, a much paler pink, and bright lavender. She waved them at me, teasingly brushing the tip of my nose, and then she set them on the dining room table and took off her jacket. Underneath, she was dressed all in black, including a black feather boa that she had sneakily tucked beneath her coat.

"Bedroom," she said, grinning, that one word setting the tone for the events of the evening. I tripped down the hall in my heels and then stood next to the bed, waiting for her next instruction.

She was right behind me, hadn't even entered the room before saying, "Now, strip." I mentally chided myself for agonizing over my attire. It was so quickly removed and tossed on the chair by the bed. Before I could ask her what to do next, she had come forward and wrapped her feather boa around my wrists. She pushed me down to a sitting position and then back so that I was sprawled on the bed. I watched as she set the feather dusters down on the pillow, then moved to position me exactly how she wanted—my legs spread apart, my bound wrists over my head, the edge of the boa caught neatly on the hook in the wall. The "handcuff hook," we call it.

"You ready?" she asked, binding my ankles to the posters of my bed with silky scarves. "Ready to be tickled until you come?"

I wanted to shake my head, but I didn't. Instead, I said, "You know I'm game, Eleanor," and then I waited for her to begin. She didn't rush into it. She never does. She always makes me wait, because she knows anticipation has a definite effect on me. The waiting makes my pussy get into the groove, makes me start to grow wet and ready even before the action begins. This time was no different. In fact, I think I got *more* wet because I really didn't know what to expect. Anticipation mixed with confusion. What an aphrodisiac.

Eleanor said, "You don't have to look so afraid. I'm not going to hurt you."

I nodded. "I know, but..." and that was all I got to say. She came forward, one feather duster in each hand, and began running the toys up and down my rib cage. I started to jerk on the boa, but Eleanor shook her head. "Careful," she said, "I don't want you to rip that." More bad news for me. How could I squirm if I had to be careful? I sent her pleading, puppy-dog looks with my eyes, but she took no pity on me. Instead, she continued with the fancy dusters, running them lightly under my armpits, then down my arms, then using one on my legs and another on my tummy. She was like an octopus, an eight-legged creature. Whenever one area of my body started to tickle too badly, she was instantly somewhere else.

"Such a good girl," she cooed, now standing by the bed and walking to the foot of it. I knew where she was going. I didn't think I'd be able to stand it.

"Oh, god," I said as she started to run the dusters up and down my bare feet. "Eleanor, I can't..." My words dissolved into helpless laughter.

"Yes, you can," she said, continuing her tickling journey. She ran the feathers over the soles of my feet, and then brushed them along the tips of my painted toenails. I couldn't heed her warning anymore. I yanked on the bindings holding my wrists to the wall. The boa snagged and bits of glossy black feathers fluttered down on top of me. But my wrists stayed bound. I bucked on the bed, raising my hips as high as I could, slamming down to the mattress each time. She'd tied my ankles tight. I was going nowhere.

My laughter rang out in the room. My body started to hurt from how hard I was giggling.

"Shhh," Eleanor admonished. Slowly, I began to give in, to let myself become overwhelmed with the tickling, taunting sensation. And giving in somehow made it bearable, although my body still shook with silent laughter. But then, that, too, began to subside, as Eleanor made her way cat-like onto the bed, moving between my legs and positioning herself right before my open cunt.

"Here?" she asked.

I took a deep, shuddering breath. I realized that I wanted to feel the feathers there. More than anything I'd ever craved before. I was dying to know what those tickling colored bits of fluff would feel like against my swollen clit.

"Please," I finally managed.

She whisked the duster over my pussy once, then slid it back again. I moaned. She took a duster in each hand and whisked back and forth, so lightly that her touch was maddening. I raised up for more pressure, but couldn't get it. She continued dusting me, lightly, gently, until my moans turned to hoarse begging sounds and the moisture in my cunt made the feathers wet.

"Come on," I begged, "I need..."

"I know what you need," Eleanor smiled at me, turning one of the dusters around to show me the smooth wooden handle. Oh, yes. That's exactly what I needed. With the same slow movements, Eleanor spread my pussylips open and lightly tapped the edge of the handle against my throbbing clit. I wasn't laughing anymore. This was no longer funny. I grit my teeth and mentally willed her to stop her teasing games. I needed fulfillment. I needed release.

Watching me carefully, my love slid the handle inside my pussy. My cunt instantly gripped onto it, squeezing as Eleanor rocked it in and out. She knows the way to do it. Oh, yes, my lover girl knows everything about what I like and how I like it. I closed my eyes, sighing gratefully, and then was rewarded as Eleanor used her free hand to tickle my clit with the turquoise duster.

The combination of the two sensations was unbelievable. My

cunt contracted on the handle of one duster as those lovely bright blue-green feathers tickled me to perfection. I floated in the bed, my head back, my hips rising up and down to the rhythm Eleanor set.

In mere moments, she had dusted me right into a electrifying orgasm. And I had shredded her feather boa by stretching it with my wrists. Eleanor looked up my body, meeting my eyes with hers.

"I've never had so much fun..." she grinned, "you know, dusting."

Next weekend is my turn. And we're going to be working on the floor in the kitchen. Until then I'm going to be wracking my brain, trying to find interesting uses for our mop.

Trust Me
by Elle McCaul

Connor invites me to a party at his house. I dress for it, in black fishnets and a short silk skirt, thinking tonight will finally be the night. This is date number four and I'm desperate to fuck him. We have that type of white-hot connection that makes me tremble whenever he touches my hand. After our last date, I couldn't fall asleep without first stroking myself, imagining it was him teasing me as I brought myself to climax.

To my dismay, the party turns out to be him and his two male roommates watching war movies all night: *Platoon, Full Metal Jacket, Patton*. I'm overdressed and underwhelmed. That is, until I notice that Connor's focused on me instead of the movie.

"Why'd you ask me here?" I whisper to him. "I mean, here with your roommates."

"I just wanted you to come over. The 'party' was an excuse."

I tilt my head and look at him, startled. "You don't need an excuse," I say softly, surprised that he can't sense how much he turns me on. "I would have come over for any reason at all. For no reason, in fact." Suddenly, he seems to get it, because his gray eyes light up and he slips one hand in mine. As in the past, the touch of his fingers sends waves of heat through me, and I blink meaningfully at him, then look over at the stairs. This is the only hint he needs.

We leave the boys in the den and go up to his bedroom. He's got a waterbed with zebra-striped sheets and he grabs me around the waist and tosses me onto it. The bed rocks beneath me and I giggle at the ride, but I have to stop laughing as he begins to undress. I've waited for this moment for over a month, and I'm more excited than I've ever been about a guy.

There is something about Connor that defies logical expectations. He's handsome, but he doesn't know it. He's a banker, but he's got a waterbed. And now, I see, as he pulls off his faded jeans and unbuttons his white shirt, that he has several tattoos, a lick of barbed wire curling around his upper bicep, a forties-style pin-up girl on his hip. His body is long and lean, and I practically lick my lips when he's down to his flannel boxers, but then I realize I'm still dressed. I'm losing this game.

Quickly, I pull my stretchy black top over my head, kick off my short skirt, and slide out of my fishnets. Then Connor takes over, undoing my lipstick red bra and pulling off my matching panties. His hands are warm and sturdy, and he could make me come in an instant if he brought his fingertips between my legs. Just touched me there. A quick circle, a firm stroke. But he doesn't. We're going to make this last. I can tell, it's going to be a night to remember.

"You look good on my bed," he says, staring at me. "Your black hair and pale skin against my sheets."

"Just like this?" I ask, stretching my arms over my head and holding the pose. I choose a position that matches the girl on his hip, and he gets it and smiles.

"As pretty as a picture."

"A moving picture," I remind him, arching my hips and beckoning with my body.

"You've been in the movies?" he wants to know, bringing his mouth, finally, *finally*, to my neck and kissing me. I can't answer right away. He has found my weakness, my all-time favorite place, and he licks and kisses in a line down my throat to my breasts. But he stops before reaching my nipples, pausing to say, "Keep talking," and I instantly understand that he wants a conversation while we fuck. He wants to play dirty.

"It was on a first date," I say.

"Bad girl."

"You have no idea." The look he gives me makes me even more excited and I grip onto his waist with my legs as he lifts me up. "I can be the baddest," I say, and he shakes his head as if he doesn't believe me. Reaching forward, I brush his light brown hair out of his eyes, and then I stare at him, daring him to break the connection.

"He had a camera and a tripod—" I tell him. "And a fantasy script that he wanted to act out."

"You were the damsel in distress and he was the hero, coming to rescue you."

"Coming," I repeat, smiling. "That part's right."

Connor grins back at me, and then resumes his kissing games, licking my lower lip, biting it so that I can't speak. His hands wander over my body and he helps me to slide onto his cock. It's the best feeling I can ever remember. The first taste of his hard rod in my dripping pussy. I forget what I was saying until he whispers, "So you had this undeniable urge to star on the silver screen?"

"No," I tell him, surprised at how normal I sound. "Not the silver screen. The TV screen." Connor is making my body hum with pleasure, and the way he moves me up and down lets me know that this ride is going to last.

"You filmed and then watched?" he asks.

"We filmed and then fucked," I tell him, "with the two of us on the TV in the background. Every once in a while, I'd look up and see myself being taken doggystyle, or sucking his cock, and it would make me excited all over again."

He shakes his head as if he can't believe I would do something like that. Not someone as sweet and innocent as I am. But looks can be deceiving, and I can tell he's reevaluating his opinion of me and that I am getting bonus points by the second. I can also tell that he wants to ask me more questions, but it's my turn to quiz him, now, and so I say, "And you? Your kinkiest time ever?"

Connor doesn't even hesitate. "She blindfolded me," he says. I don't know who "she" was, and for once I don't care. I'm not jealous of the ghost lovers in Connor's past. But I am curious.

"Did you like it?" I ask.

"At first. She said 'Trust me,' and then she tied a black silk scarf over my eyes and made me promise not to peek. She staged a sort of quiz show, rubbing these different objects over my—" he hesitates before saying 'cock,' which I think is sort of cute since I'm bouncing on it.

"Then what?" I ask, breathing hard.

"I had to guess what the item was before she tried another one."

"What did she rub on you?"

"A stuffed animal. A wooden coaster. A CD." He runs his fingers up and down my ribs, almost absentmindedly. His sturdy hands move up, finding my nipples, and he lightly pinches them between thumb and forefinger, making them hard in an instant. I'm learning quickly that Connor is one of those casual lovemakers who is very, very good. I can barely remember what I'm supposed to say next, but he reminds me.

"Have you ever done anything like that?"

I shake my head and my long, dark hair brushes my shoulders. Never. "What happened?" I'm panting. "What did she do next?"

"She rubbed something cold and hard against me."

He's rubbing something warm and hard between my legs. The talking part of this game is getting more difficult. "And it was?" I finally manage to murmur. My voice no longer sounds like me. It's a hungry whispering sound, an animal, a porn star.

"I couldn't guess."

"So she kept rubbing?"

He sighs and nods. "She said, 'Trust me,' and she just kept going."

"And you didn't have any idea?" I'm thinking, cold and hard. A metal spoon. A cucumber. A Popsicle.

"I knew," he says, pushing up with his hips so that I buck forward. I grip into his shoulders to keep myself steady and I start to work my body more seriously against his. The feel of his cock, slicked up with my juices, is making it difficult for me to stay focused. But I'm a competitive type of girl. I hate to lose at anything. So I force myself to continue.

"You didn't want to guess?"

"I knew what it was," he continues, "I just didn't want to believe it. I couldn't make myself say the word."

I slide back and forth on him. Oh, man, is he good. I could keep riding and riding, except that now he's working his hand down my flat belly, finding just the right spot between my legs to flick with his fingertips. His fingers make tiny circles that miss my clit on purpose. I shift my hips to make a connection, but he continues to play his teasing tricks. Circles that come within a breath of where I need them and then flicker off course. Just out of reach. He's driving me crazy, which is definitely the point. Still, I'm almost there.

"What was it?" I whisper, about to reach the top.

"A knife," he says, "a butcher knife. She was running the flat side of it up and down my cock. Not playing with the blade, but letting me feel that cool, smooth surface. When I finally had the guts to say it aloud, she put the knife down, climbed on top of me, and fucked the living daylights out of me."

The image makes him seem both vulnerable and strong, powerless and powerful, and this is what makes me come. I don't know why, but it does.

"And after?" I ask him softly. He's still inside me, and I can tell by the look in his deep gray eyes that he's almost reached his peak. His cock throbs within my pussy, going deeper still, deeper than I thought possible. Another stroke, another plunge, and he'll be there.

"We broke up," he says through clenched teeth. "I mean, if she could do something like that on a whim, how could I ever trust her?"

He's bigger than me, so strong, and he grips me around the waist and pulls me even harder onto him, sealing our bodies together and groaning as he reaches that place, that fantasy place, and lets loose.

Downstairs, in the den, I can hear rockets go off.

Underwater
by Emilie Paris

My days are long and lazy. I hang out at the beach with the skate rats and the surfers, the boys who bake beneath the rays, not caring where the next rent check is coming from. The young sun gods all live together, crashed out in a big house by the ocean, thirteen or fourteen youths sharing one phone, mattresses on the floors and in the hallways. Their house needs a paint job, but they don't care. The front steps are battered, broken, but they sit on them anyway, kicking their bare feet up on the wall and watching the sunset. The surf stars don't seem to have visible means of support, but somehow they always manage to scrounge up the rent money by the end of the month. It appears, like magic, finding its way into the envelope they hand over to their bemused landlord.

I don't worry about rent either, but I don't have to. I've got a high-paying job, one that works me to a near-breaking point for months on end and then releases me for much-needed regrouping. If you live in Los Angeles, you know people like me. Movie people. We power-work night and day on a film, then relax until the phone rings again. But unlike the faces on the screen, I'm not well-known. I've never been linked in the tabloids to any celebrity. When I have free time, I can hide among the riffraff without being recognized. That's how it is when you're the eye behind the camera. Only those truly in the know can pick me out of a crowd.

So, in the days after a movie is finished, I pull my favorite faded 501s from the closet, snag a tank top left by a long-gone lover, slip on my wayfarers, and hit the shimmering sidewalk at Venice Beach. I buy a soft serve vanilla ice cream cone and lick it as I make my way to the ramp where the rats are jumping. When I get close, I find a shady spot beneath a palm tree, and sit down to watch the boys do their tricks. From my regular location, I can keep track of both the skate-boarders on their ramps and the surfers as they dive and dance among the waves. It thrills me, watching the kings of the beach kick-ass on their respective slats, the skaters going upside-down over nothing but concrete, the surfers slicing through the waves.

Other girls gather around, too, summertime chicklets clad in brightly colored string bikinis or sheer, halter-style dresses. They "ooh" and "ahhh" at each fabulous trick, at each display of testosterone. These girls bring iced sodas and snacks and rub suntan lotion on the broad-shouldered backs of the weary beach boys. I never get quite that involved. If I want to make an impression, I leave the picnic stuff at home. When I see someone I want, I take off my sunglasses and wait.

I'm not as young as most of the gang. I'm 28, which is ancient by Hollywood standards, but I have a thin, tight-muscled body, can pass for a co-ed when I need to. My strawberry blonde hair is long in front, with bangs I peek out from under. I scrape it off my face and into a sleek ponytail when I'm working, but "off" times, I wear it hanging free, down to my sharp shoulder blades in back and to the tips of my eyelashes in front. In the summer, my hair gets lighter, bleaches out in streaks to give me that true California girl look. I don't cultivate the image, but it serves the purpose when I want it to.

I have blue eyes, blue like the sky without any smog, clear and intense. When I take off my sunglasses, my eyes are what guys notice first. That is, if they haven't seen me smile. My smile is a grabber. I have teeth like Bowie's, small, animal teeth. Guys see me grin and instantly have visions of my teeth sinking into their naked skin. I know how to leave just the right marks, not too deep. Little reminders of a wild night, a whirlwind romance in the shadows of a sand dune. My love bites are souvenirs, and I think my partners are always sad when the last remnants of my incisors fade away.

Some of my friends would be shocked by my tastes. I simply don't look the part of the dominatrix. I'm slight, but I'm tough. My lovers have always submitted to my needs. There's never been a question about it. I call to them, the ones that like to bow down. I don't seek them out, they come to me.

But *I* come to the boys of summer. I am drawn to the way they flip up in the air. Pulled in by the tricks they do. Captivated by their gravity-defying moves. I align myself with that free-flying attitude. These heavenly contenders don't care about pain. If they fall down, they get back the fuck up again, and do it over. And *over*. They have scars on their slim bodies from accidents past. They have tattoos, like colorful birthmarks, wrapped around their arms, legs, decorating their skin like splashes of paint on tautly stretched canvases.

I appreciate them, and they know it. I'm different from the bimbos in bikinis. I have a power that they sense. I can make them blush simply by watching them play, and my presence somehow brings out their best. They land all their moves when I'm nearby, watching. They shine when I'm around.

I don't take the dare devils the way I take other men. I have sex with them, sure, but I don't conquer them. I let their moves steal over us both. I let them turn my bed into a playground, a jungle gym, and take over from there. Or I find myself in their beds, playing by their rules, which is infinitely easy because they have none.

That's how I know about the mattresses in the hallways. It's how I know about the single phone and the shared bathroom. I have found myself in an arched-back position on more than one of those mattresses, watching my reflection in a window at the end of the long, narrow hallway. No sheet beneath me, just the blue-and-white striped ticking of an old navy bedroll. None of the niceties you'd find in the apartments of the movie folks I work with. No bedside table displaying a fashionable artsy lamp. No signed and framed Nagel over the leather sofa in the living room.

I don't like those things, don't need them.

What I need is some nineteen-year-old, golden-skinned boy behind me, a twisted, faded friendship band around his wrist and nothing else on his perfect body. In the window-mirror, I see that his eyes are closed, but I watch. We do it doggystyle, with me on all fours and him on his knees in back of me. He holds onto my hips, impales me, moves to a beat he can hear in his head.

I try to hear that same beat. I rock my body forward and back. I like the way his rough hands feel on my skin, like the way his tanned body looks against my pale figure. I can see that in the window, but I can't see the color of his eyes, because they're closed. And I can't hear the music that he hears, because he's young and in the groove of summertime and skate rat dreams. And to him, I'm this little blonde chick he met on the beach that he wanted to go upside-down with.

But I'm a grownup, a voice says in my head, and I can't lose myself in the moves anymore. I am present while he fucks me. My mind doesn't take off on a fantasy trip. I feel his fingers digging into my skin. I hear his breath coming in a rush. I know that he's trying to keep himself from shooting too soon when he moves back, when he turns me on the mattress so I'm on my side, and he's in me from behind, spooning this time. Those calloused fingertips find my clit and rub, getting me up to his speed, helping me to forget myself and learn the rhythm of his choosing. His fingers are knowledgeable. They sense to dart into my pussy and get wet and slippery with my liquid sex. They know to rub over my clit, over and over, then around and around. I am in love with the touch of his fingers. I lean back against his chest and shut my eyes.

In my mind, I can picture our bodies together. I see us like a painting, his dark burnished skin to my pale body, his short, scruffy goatee framing an impish smile, his light eyes an oasis shimmering in the heat. We could be a graffiti painting on the outside of one of the warehouses near the beach, a sprawling vision by some barrio artist, combining colors and lights and shadows.

He moves me again, whispering something, his mouth pressed against my ear, saying, "How do you like it, baby? How do you like it?"

I roll onto my back and look at him, memorizing the lines of his face. I smile at him when he opens his eyes, green-gray eyes that seem glazed as he stares back at me. He asks it again, "How do you like it?" Then, "How do you need it?" Stressing that one word. Need.

I can't tell him, so I say, "Just like this," as he climbs on top of me, starts doing push-ups over my body, the muscles in his fine arms bulging. He teases me with the head of his cock between my lightly furred pussy lips, pulling out, all the way out so that I'm stretching, straining to reach him, and then giving me a shy sort of naughty grin and slipping just the tip back in again. I squeeze him with my muscles, try to drain him with my power. He's good, though. He makes the most of the ride, whatever the ride may be, whether he's skimming the surf on a neon-painted boogie board. Whether he's doing those death-defying moves on a skate ramp with no safety net, or going upside-down with me on his mattress.

He says, "Talk to me, baby... tell me what you like."

Could I tell him that I like *him*? That I like his spirit, and that I see it when he rides his board. I don't think so. I would sound phony. I would sound old, trying to capture a bit of his youth and make it my own. But it is what I like. His strong body against mine. The way his hair smells of wind and sea spray and his skin actually tastes of summertime, of heat.

He croons, "Tell me, baby, talk to me."

I shake my head, still trying to pull him inside me, to keep him inside me, my pussy making a juicy, kissing sound each time he rocks in and out. I turn it around. I say, "I like it like this. Just like this. But tell me. You tell me what you like."

He's got his answer ready. He was waiting the whole time. Still working me, without missing a beat, he says, "It sends me when a girl says my name as she's coming."

Then he bends and starts to kiss the underside of my jawline, the hollow of my neck. He tickles me with the pointy tip of his tongue and I almost laugh. He takes hold of my wrists and pins them over my head and then moves down my body to kiss my small breasts, licking and sucking with his ravenous mouth. His cock is pressed up against my leg, slick and wet from the juices of my sex, but I can tell he's not going to enter me again until I ask what needs to be asked.

I strain to see if he'll hold me down, and he does. And then, awful as it may sound, I confess, "I don't know your name."

"My name's on my body. It's like a treasure hunt... see if you can find it." Then he lets go of my wrists and stands up, leaning against the wall, regarding me with a look of total satisfaction.

He's like a statue. Still, absolutely still, his cock straining out and away from him. His eyes, half-closed, let me know he has all the time we need. I look up the line of his body, seeing the different tattoos, the different marks and scars. I sit up on my heels, begin tracing the designs with my tongue. He turns, slowly, his face to the wall now, and I see the black-inked word on his lower back: Eden. I start to say it, but he turns around again quickly, shaking his head at me, coming back down on the mattress, moving us so that I am over him, riding him, my body split at the middle, my legs pumping, keeping him deep inside me. I move without thinking, without planning. I am on him, sliding up and down his cock with graceful ease, not doing it because he wants it or I want it, but doing it because it's right.

"When you come," he says, his voice hoarse, letting me know how it's going to be. "Say it when you come."

I ride him hard. I don't let his cock slip out of me again, but I pound myself on it, fucking him now. This is how I'm used to doing it, holding my partner down with my will alone, my body easy and light. But he's different. He's not in it to be overpowered. He's in it to watch my face change when I come. He's in it for the experience, for that heart-stopping feeling of reaching your peak and looking down from the sky above. Making love to him lets me see the world as he does, see what it would be like to ride the waves, to feel the board beneath my feet and duck through a tunnel of blue-green sun-drenched water.

He trails his fingers over my cheekbones. He presses his thumb against my bottom lip. I lick it, draw it into my mouth, suck on his thumb while I fuck him. He sighs. His body shifts beneath me, my still-pumping legs, my sweat-slicked thighs. He grabs hold of my waist and moves me so that we are on our sides, facing each other, staring into each others' eyes.

And then I move my head, look over his shoulder, and see his roommates in the other room. There the whole time. I freeze for one moment, stop moving against Eden. I'm startled by their presence, but they smile at me, grinning to show how easy-going they are. Their bodies are tanned and strong. The five of them drink lemonade and inhale clove cigarettes, blowing wispy breaths of fragrant smoke toward the ceiling.

I don't smile when I see them, but I feel elated. The group gazes at us as if we're a movie put on for their sole pleasure. They view us in the same manner they watch other athletes at the beach, genuinely impressed with the show. Letting someone else entertain them. I come from seeing them there, from the audience, from the youth of the boys around me. It brings me down for just a moment, holds me under for just long enough to get off.

Eden feels those vibrations around his cock, and he starts to move his hands on my body, up my slender waist toward my breasts, stroking me all over, coming with me and playing me to make it last. I have seen him carry his skateboard with that same amount of gentleness, or roughness, or some combination of the two that shows how much he appreciates it. I come and collapse against him, the warmth of our bodies complimentary, the warmth in the room and in the glowing eyes of our audience a small fire of purity.

I'm underwater. His touch brings me back to the surface.

I'm not sure how much I like being up above, able to breathe free again, to see the crescent moon through the window, to see the hazy smoke clouds the skate rats exhale with each breath. I'd rather be under, held down, his body on mine, topsy-turvy in a slick and sweaty sixty-nine, his warm cock in my mouth, my pussy throbbing under his tongue. The sweet, sweat-salt taste of his skin a mixture of hard work and a bath in the sea after a long day's ramping. I know the feel of him pressing into me, pushing me back down under the waves. I trail my fingers along the tribal design of a blue-inked tattoo that is a part of him, the ink like blood in the veins pounding under his skin.

I say, "I forgot..." but he just looks at me. I tilt my head back, arch my body on the mattress, wanting his tongue down there, between my legs, and he nods as he turns his body so that his face is between my thighs and his cock, wet and dripping from my sex, is poised just over my lips. Knowing that others are watching makes me shiver inside. I open my mouth and he slides in. I suck on him, drink from him, roll my tongue around his straining rod, so well-oiled with my own wetness. I'm gone again, deep under his body, deep under water, pressed down into the mattress, loving him with my mouth while he plays in and out games with his tongue in my pussy.

I've had many different lovers taking me over the edge, but my mind never truly goes on hold unless I'm with one of the boys of summer. Someone like Eden, with the scars he wears like badges of honor, with the tattoos saved hard for and paid for in cash. He'll never grow up. Maybe that's what I like most about him. He'll get older, but his heart will always be alert and alive, doing back flips off a homemade ramp without any fear of the ground rushing up from below.

I hear the waves outside, crashing against the sand. He hears the ocean, too, and uses the rhythm of the surf in the way he kisses me, finding my clit between his lips and sucking on it to that beat. Hard and then soft, lapping for a moment, and then suckling again. He knows how to do it. He knows just how to give the most pleasure, taking me upward until I have a view of the very top, before sliding me back down again. I break and crest. I ride the peaks and valleys. I forget who I am, what I do, what language I speak. I know only one thing, his name, and I say it over and over, his cock still in my mouth, the word slurred.

I say, "Eden," just as he asked me to, just as he told me to. I say, "E-den," dragging out his name, making it last. I'm underwater when I reach it. I hold my breath, hear my heart pounding in my ears. I feel faint, dizzy, spreading my legs wide apart, my head tossed back, my hips thrusting forward. I shake with the climax, letting out my air, finally, taking a deep, shuddering breath in, finding the surface and breaking free.

Vulcan Mindblower
by Mary Jo Vaughn

I'm not even sure if that's the right name for it. Maybe you know. Maybe you've had one. Those iced pink drinks served in Martini glasses at Jezebelle's on 13th Street. They're mean, they are. They'll blow you away. I'm not a lightweight. Don't even let that thought enter your head. I can do Tequila Body Shots all night long. But the Mindblowers, they're different. They sneak the fuck up on you when you're not looking, when you're not thinking much except, "Mmmm... that was good. I'll have another."

I was in that sort of a state when Mira found me. I was leaning up against the cool, wood bar of Jezebelle's, my face flushed, my dark hair pulled high off my neck and captured there with a sterling silver clip. I had on a black turtleneck that I'd just freed from storage and it smelled a bit like the sachet I'd tucked into the box: faded roses and baby powder. A comfort smell.

Mira glided up behind me. I didn't notice her until I saw her reflection in the blue-tinted mirror behind the bar. She said, "Buy you the next?"

I didn't turn toward her, simply steeled myself and met her eyes in the mirror. She looked clear and crisp, her short white-blonde hair slicked back, her gray-green eyes razor sharp, even in the dim light of the bar.

"You bet," I said, nodding, feeling her hand snake down the back of my loose 501s. She was checking to see if I had on panties. I didn't.

The bartender replaced my dead drink with a new one, and Mira turned sideways and watched me down it. When I'd finished, she grabbed my hand and led me down the dark hallway to the ladies' room.

"You smell like sex," she said, under her breath, as she pulled me along.

"Roses and baby powder," I corrected her, taking a whiff of my sweater.

She pulled me after her into the ladies' room and locked the door behind us.

"And sex," she said again, pulling the turtleneck over my head, propping me up against the sink while she pulled my jeans down, leaving them on me.

The sink was cold against my naked ass, but her hands were warm as they spread my cunt lips, and her mouth was hot as she pressed it against me. I liked the feel of the metal ball that rides her tongue as she tickled my clit with it. Warm mouth and cool silver combined can start a fire within me. Mira knows that well.

I held onto the edge of the sink, kicked off my shoes, and waited for her to pull my jeans all the way off. Then, balancing most of my weight on the sink, I wrapped my slender legs around her, capturing her to me, capturing her face to my cunt. If she wanted to play, we'd play my way, drunk though I was.

I loved the feeling of that silver ball rolling back and forth over my clit, then icing my insides as she used her tongue like a cock and probed me deeper. Mira knows what to do. Yes, she does.

There are two mirrors in Jezebelle's ladies' room, and I stared in the one across the way to watch my face as I came. I moved again, so I was standing, and I placed my hands on the back of Mira's shaved neck and jammed her hard against me, rolling her with the vibrations that swelled inside me and cascaded over. I bounced back and forth, slamming my ass against the rim of the sink and then forward, into her face, and she punished me for the intensity of my movements by digging that silver ball right into the throbbing heat of my clit, spiraling me into a violent world of painandpleasureandpainandpleasure... and pain.

"Hurts so good," she grinned at me when she stood up, wiping her mouth on the back of her hand, "doesn't it?"

"It always does when you ride the helm," I agreed, staring into her clear eyes and waiting.

"I miss you," she said next, working hard to get that hurt look to her face that doesn't belong on it. Mira doesn't feel any real emotions, so far as I can tell. And after dating her for four years and recently being the one to instigate the breakup, I should know.

"Miss me," I said as I left her alone in the bathroom. I poked my head in for one last dig, "But thanks for the climax. It was great."

What She Likes...
by Ann Blakely

I've always wanted to be with a woman. Never did it before. Never had the guts, or the opportunity, in that order. Yeah, I heard a lot of rumors about girls playing together in college, sweaty under-the-sheets and under-the-skirt explorations. But I guess I was on the no-lesbian floor, because nothing so pleasurably kinky ever happened between me and my uptight blonde roommate.

After dorm life, I hooked up with several long-term boyfriends, one right after the other until I got married, so I missed out on any experimentation in my early twenties and made do with fantasies instead. Different women starred in my X-rated mental movies. Jo from the television show "The Facts of Life." Angelina Jolie in just about every film she's ever been in. And this intensely good-looking room service waitress who brought food to my suite in an upscale San Francisco hotel. Dark hair cut short, pale skin, jade-colored eyes. She gave me a look as she placed the tray of food on the table by my bed, a defiant, "I dare you" look that fueled my fantasies for months. How I wanted her to serve me something entirely different from the luke-warm bowl of soup she set down—

But I was straight, so what was I doing having these thoughts? Nothing except coming to them, my delicate fingertips slick and wet as they plunged between my shaved pussy lips, my body arched in an S-curve on the mattress until I couldn't handle it anymore. I needed to own the reality. Needed a woman not only in my head, but in my bed.

Confessing the fantasy to my husband turned out to be the easy part. I should have known. All guys seem to like the thought of their girl with another chick. Adam was probably just waiting for me to suggest it first so that he didn't come across as a cad.

"I want to fuck a woman," I told him late one night, curled up so that my body was pressed tight against his beneath the sheets, my face half-hidden in the pillow.

"While I watch?"

"While you join in."

"You'd like that?" he asked me seriously as I felt his cock harden against my thigh. "Tell me about it, Lauren. Tell me what you'd like—"

Whispering to him about all the filthy things I hoped to do with a woman was simple. I told him how I desperately wanted to know what another girl's juices would taste like. Thick like cream? Sharp and tangy? I knew my own flavor from sucking Adam's rod after he'd been inside of me, or from kissing him after we'd sixty-nined. But that wasn't good enough any longer. I wanted the scent and the taste of a real woman's cunt on my lips.

Throughout that evening, I explained to Adam how I'd press my mouth against her soft pussy skin, how I'd take her throbbing clit between my teeth. I had a feeling I would be an expert at pleasing a female lover. Didn't I already know all the tricks that I like best? Those endless spirals that almost touch that pulsing pleasure point but slide away before making contact. The rapid, flutters that work me right through an orgasm. Wouldn't I be just perfect at giving a woman head?

Adam seemed to think so.

"Tell me again, Lauren," he requested as he rolled on top of me in our bed. "Tell me what you'd like—" he urged as he pushed the sheets away and pressed the head of his cock between my slicked-up pussy lips. I could feel how hard he was, how excited at the thought of what I was describing.

"My mouth on her," I murmured. "My fingers holding her pussy lips wide open, like this, tongue thrusting deep up in there. Sliding inside her. Tickling and stroking. My hands cradling her ass, spreading her cheeks apart, touching her back there. Lightly. Softly. Probing and thrusting."

As I spoke, Adam fucked me, getting more into it the dirtier I talked. He came ferociously as I finished sharing my full-on fantasy. And I knew from the way he stared down at me with sex-glazed eyes that he was game. We were going to have to find a girl to fuck.

But while picturing the acts came naturally, finding a willing partner turned out to be more difficult. We were at a loss as to how to proceed. Should we go to one of those clubs that advertised at the back of *The Weekly*? Doll ourselves up and try to blend in with the other swingers? That didn't seem like our style. After careful consideration, we placed a well-worded ad in the paper:

What she likes...
Is the thought of another woman in bed.
Of becoming a sexual sandwich between
her man and her new girlfriend.
What she needs...
Is to turn this fantasy into a reality.
Attractive Married White Couple seeks
nymphet with know-how.

But as soon as our kindly provided voice mailbox was filled, we had a new problem. Where would we interview those who responded? Can't give strangers your phone number or home address, not even strangers you want to screw. To lick and suck. To push down between your legs and feel their kitten-like tongues on your clit. Finally, we chose a hot spot by the Bay, an upscale place where the other diners would have no idea that we were interviewing for a third bedmate.

"My dogs are barking," girl number one said as she slid into the emerald green leather booth. She had the right look. Not too slutty. Just slutty enough. As a natural redhead, I have always had a thing for brunettes, and I liked her tousled dark hair, the violet smudges of exhaustion under her ocean-blue eyes, as if she'd been up fucking for a week.

Turned out, she had. And as she went into extreme detail about the way the new guy in her life had ass-fucked her up against the railing on her wrap-around balcony, Adam and I both came silently to the same conclusion: This girl was too much for us. As novices, we wouldn't have minded hooking up with someone who had a little experience. But Leslie, well, she could have taught classes on the subject of threesomes, foursomes, orgies and more.

Next up was a girl who didn't much like men, to put it mildly. I shouldn't call her a girl, I guess, but a womyn—someone who said "goddess" instead of "god" and "herstory" instead of "history." She explained that she chose not to use the "white man's language," and at first, I couldn't fathom why she had answered our ad. We'd been straight-forward in explaining that we were a hetero couple in search of a feline female friend. Then I realized that this interviewee was hoping to woo me away from both my man and men in general. She'd answered our ad simply to tell me that the males of this species were no damn good. As she went into extreme detail about her nearly violent disregard for the opposite sex, my husband quite openly began to fear for his penis, and he shook his head repeatedly at me to let me know that this gyrl simply wasn't right for us.

As the evening progressed, I started to feel like a sex-crazed Goldilocks. The first woman was too hot. The second too cold. Would the third be just right? Of course she would, because this particular fairy tale has a happy ending.

For our final interview of the night, we spoke with Kiki. Perfect name. Feminine-sounding to balance the way she looked in her sleek leather pants and tight white T-shirt, like Joan Jett from her years with the Runaways. I tried to keep my eyes on her face—sharp cheekbones, strong chin—but my gaze was captivated by her pert breasts beneath that spandex shirt. I visualized sucking on her nipples, pinching them, stroking my thumbs over the hardened nubs and then grazing the tips with my teeth. She didn't seem to mind my lecherous gaze, giving me a wink as she told us that she was a web designer in the city. Cresting thirty, she was just my age, yet she seemed so much more relaxed in this erotic interview environment, while every single gesture she made brought a new sex-charged image to my mind.

To my further delight, Kiki had a considerate way of looking over at Adam to be sure he felt included in our conversation, even though most of the time it was us girls talking. Sharing stories, secrets, doing the flirtatious dance that I'd forgotten about. When you've been married for a few years, you leave those sexy little steps behind. The head tilt, up-from-under look, lower lip lick. I remembered right away with Kiki. I might have been slow at first, but I figured it all out.

"You want excitement," Kiki said, resting one hand on mine. She was making a statement, not asking a question, but I answered it anyway.

"I want to know if it's the same."

She looked at me, obviously not understanding.

"If the real thing is the same as the fantasy."

Now she got it, and she shook her head, dark hair falling away from her face to reveal an open, honest expression in her clear gray eyes. I felt disappointment welling inside me until she continued quietly. "Not the same, Lauren," she promised, "but much, much better."

Adam squeezed my thigh tightly under the table, then took my free hand and pressed my palm against the crotch of his faded jeans so that I could feel the hardness of his hidden erection. We had a mutual 'yes' vote, and I quickly invited our new playmate to our place, but she suggested her apartment instead. "It's close," she told us. "Less than a mile."

We followed Kiki to her bay-view condo. She waited for us on the landing with a smile on her face, looking just like any hostess greeting her guests. But once inside, I felt a crazy moment of panic at what to do next. Or what to do *first*. We'd all agreed to fuck— that was a given—but this was completely different from any other sexual experience I'd had. With boys at school, I'd let them lead, and it wasn't until we'd found ourselves on a bed, or sofa, or stretch of green grass between two hulking lecture halls, that I'd make my desires known. With Adam, I didn't even have to say what I needed any longer. He sensed automatically when I wanted him to dominate me, when I was in the mood for getting a bare-bottom spanking over his sturdy lap, or being cuffed to our brass-railed headboard. Now, in a room with three people, each with a personal, private agenda, I was momentarily lost.

Lost, that is, until Kiki made the first move. "You'd think it would be easy," she said as she kicked off her boots, then slowly unzipped her form-fitting leather jeans and slid them down her taut, toned thighs. "We all know how this evening is going to end. There's none of that 'will she put out or won't she?' drama. And still, everyone winds up tongue-tied."

Without the slightest hint of self-consciousness, she pulled her T-shirt over her head, revealing small, round breasts captured by a white lacy bra that matched her panties. Cocking a hip, she continued, "Being tongue-tied is fine, you know. There's no reason to speak right now."

Saying this, she came toward me and slowly undid the buttons running the length of my black dress. With her help, I was soon down to my own matching panty set, an expensive French underwire bra and black bikinis. When I looked over at Adam, he seemed stunned by the vision before him: two pretty young women in nothing but their panties. What more could any man want? Or any woman....

Kiki took a moment to observe me, and then she smiled before grabbing my hand and leading me toward her bedroom. Adam followed, as she must have known he would, tossing his clothes in a trail after him. In the bedroom, the feeling was an echo of what it had been at the bar. Kiki included Adam, sweetly, with a motion of her head letting him know that he should join us in the center of her queen-sized bed. Once there, she spread me out between the two of them and said simply, "Show me what she likes."

Adam had no problem being a teacher. Bending down, he licked me through my panties, using the flat of his tongue against my pussy so that I could feel the warm wetness through the black lace. He played me up and down for several seconds before looking at Kiki with his deep brown eyes. "She likes the barrier at first, being sucked through the material before I take off her knickers."

"I can do that," Kiki said, "while you lick her nipples and get them all hard." I shivered deliciously at the fact that they were speaking about me as if I weren't there. It was oddly erotic, having two people discuss what I liked and making plans about who would do what to which location as if I were some sexual road map and they were charting an afternoon's outdoor excursion.

Then Kiki was between my legs, taking over from Adam, licking up the seam of my panties, pressing her mouth against my pussy lips and letting me feel the delicious, wet heat of her tongue.

"You'll like it better when I get these off," she said, "because I'm going to finger-fuck you, and then I'm going to tongue-fuck your pussy until you scream." And that's what I immediately needed. For her to take my panties off me, to pull them down and discard them. To slide her fingers up inside my snatch and touch me from the inside out. Adam was busy removing my bra and then suckling with his mouth on my nipples, but I didn't even notice that anymore. I was desperately waiting for Kiki to do as she'd just described.

Luckily, she didn't make me wait long.

"Now, Adam," she said, "I have a bag of toys on the top shelf in the hall closet. Why don't you go get them and bring them back here." I realized what she was doing before he did. She was getting rid of him for the moment, wanting to spend time with only me. But Adam didn't care. This was my fantasy. He was happily willing to play a part in it, but he didn't need to be the star. As soon as he was out of the room, Kiki had my panties down and my pussy lips spread. She started as she'd promised, one finger up inside me, then two, and then she brought her mouth to my cunt and began to tickle my clit with the tip of her tongue.

Oh, Jesus, it felt good. The way she trailed circles over my clit with her tongue while her fingers were fucking me harder and faster, back and forth. Adam returned to the room as Kiki slid her body around in a sixty-nine, and I looked between her thighs to see him leaning against the wall and watching, stunned, at the porno movie that had suddenly come to life for him, with his wife in the lead role.

My first fantasy came true right then. With my mouth on Kiki's pussy, I eased apart her pussy lips and tasted the liquid sex within. Her juices were different from mine. Sweeter? Darker? I slid my tongue in further, wanting another swallow. Wanting the nectar smeared over my mouth, my cheeks, making the skin on my face glisten. I suddenly realized that Kiki was mimicking me, gracefully using her fingers and tongue on my naked pussy, rubbing the point of her tongue in a circle around the ridge of my clit, before thrusting it deep inside my body. I thought she'd make me come in a minute simply by continuing with that same back and forth rhythm. A flick of her tongue on my clit, followed by a long deep stroke within, but Kiki had other ideas.

"What else does she like, Adam?" Kiki murmured, staring over her shoulder at my husband. Her fingers were still playing music within me, probing and teasing, and I wanted to tell her not to stop. Just to keep on doing what she was doing. But then Adam said, "She likes it when I put her over my knee—" And that was all Kiki needed to know.

"A spanking?" she asked, sitting up quickly and then looking down at me with an evil grin. "So you like to be a bad girl, do you?"

I think I nodded. I'm not sure. I wanted to answer in the way that would get me what I craved, which was now to be over Kiki's lap, to feel her hand connecting with my bare ass, to be on display for Adam while a woman spanked me.

"Hand me the paddle," she told Adam, speaking like a doctor to an assistant. Not scalpel, but *paddle*. Adam rummaged through the bag of toys he'd brought at her request into the room, and then he quickly gave her the implement she was hoping for.

"Over my knee," Kiki said, moving to the edge of the bed and waiting. It was a long crawl for me to roll over and position myself in proper spanking form across her lap. My face was flushed a rose-pink from embarrassment as well as the closeness I already was to coming. Kiki didn't seem to notice. She simply lifted the black and red Ping-Pong paddle and brought it down hard against my bare ass. It made a loud sound to accompany the instant stinging sensation, but all I did was grind my hips against her lap, and raise my butt up higher, wanting to feel it again.

"Oh, you are a bad girl," Kiki crooned. "You want more. You want me to spank you harder, to spank you until you come."

That's exactly what I wanted. Kiki let the paddle smack against me a second time, a third, and then she set the toy down, parted my cheeks and used her bare fingers to slap against my pussy. Fucking Christ, it was amazing. Her fingers made a dreamy sound as they found the wetness of my cunt. She was going to spank me to climax. I was sure of it, until she said to Adam, "What else?"

He didn't answer right away. I think he was in shock.

"Tell me what she likes—" Kiki demanded.

Finally, he said, "She likes it when I fuck her asshole after a spanking."

"Mmm," Kiki sighed, as if considering it. I was thrilled when she said, "Okay, you'll do that while I fuck her pussy. Hand me the dildo." Adam found a hot pink plastic cock and showed that to Kiki, but she shook her head. "The battery-powered one with the harness." After another moment, he found what she wanted, and then he came forward, joining us on the bed.

"Take her doggy-style," Kiki said, sliding the leather harness around her waist, and then slipping easily beneath me on the mattress, her body slender and flexible. I felt her cock enter my pussy just as Adam spread my asscheeks and placed the tip of his penis against my asshole. A sandwich, that's what I was going to be. A sex sandwich, between this lovely brunette and my willing husband. I couldn't contain the moans that welled from deep within me as Adam and Kiki got into the same rhythm, him thrusting, then pulling almost all of the way out as she bucked her hips into me, then turned on the vibrator.

Now, Adam was the one to moan, feeling the mechanical rumblings work through my body to him. He fucked harder, and I found myself crying out at the pleasure as it slammed through me. I'd never felt anything so decadent before. Skin on skin, Kiki's firm breasts pressed into me below, Adam's lean body on mine from behind.

Kiki came first, her pussy pressed hard against the base of the vibrator, getting off on being the one on the bottom. Adam was next, shooting his river of come deep inside of my ass and sighing my name as the vibrations flowed through him. Caught between the two of them, my orgasm was stretched out, the vibrator still on inside my cunt, making it last. The heat of our bodies sealed us together and we stayed in that position for several minutes, regaining our selves and our sense of accomplishment at the same time.

This was it. That magical moment I'd waited for all those years, dreaming about as I played with myself or as my husband played with me. A night of new discovery to remember—

Kiki broke through my sappy poetic thoughts. Looking over at Adam, she grinned, slipping quickly out of the harness and propping herself up on one elbow at my side. "And for the second round," she said, her fingers playing lightly over my flat belly before moving lower, "Tell me what she likes...."

X-Rated Conversations
by Becky Chapel

"Baby, you ready?"

So ready. I've been waiting for this call, dressed in my pale green silk negligee, my hair rustling in lustrous curls past my shoulders, my skin still warm and buffed from a day on the beach. I've been in bed with a fashion magazine open before me—not reading, not even looking at the pictures of silky, feline women—just turning the pages and waiting.

"Stefanie-girl . . ." Giselle continues, "Take your panties down, take them down to your ankles and bend over on the bed."

I do it without thinking, ignoring the voice in my head that taunts me, *"She's not here, not really, you can just pretend."* That's a lie. I do it because she *is* here, throwing me forward on the bed and bending on her knees to eat me from behind—thrusting her pink tongue between my porcelain thighs and drinking from the split of my body. She *is* here with me, commanding me to spread my legs wider, to bend over further, and I do it, hands clutching the phone, breathing ragged, heartbeat exploding in my ears.

"Turn over," she orders, and I'm with her, her hands gripping into my waist, lifting me off the bed with each forward drive of her hips, each thrust impaling me with her strap-on cock. "That's the girl," she says, her voice urgent, "Oh, how beautiful you are." Her fingers trail along my belly, up to my breasts, cupping them, teasing my nipples, just brushing the tips. She anchors me with her body, the weight of her body on top of mine, and she leans forward to kiss me, slow and long, her skin warm on my own, her lips smooth and dry. We're so close together that I feel her heartbeat link with my own. It's like music, the way we move, the rhythm of the dance. It's like fire, the glow in her eyes, the heat of her skin.

It's like she's here with me.

"C'mon, Stefanie, kiss me, darling."

My head tilts against the cool satin of my pillow, my lips part, as if I am kissing a demon lover, a phantom, an incubus. My body rocks beneath hers, invisible, unreal, and then the currents work through me.

I can picture her in my mind, her pale curls, like an angel's, her eyes shut tight, the blonde lashes against her tanned skin. Her mouth is tense, canine teeth biting into her bottom lip, the urgency creasing her sculptured face. She arches her head back as she moans aloud—the image of ecstasy. I bask in the sublime look that crosses her face as she reaches the climax. I own that look.

"Darling," Giselle sighs, her breathing gone dark and heavy. "That was amazing."

"Yes . . ."

"Call me tomorrow . . ." she whispers, no talk of her day—of mine—of the work that separates us.

"Yes," another sigh, filled with satisfaction. "Yes, Giselle. Tomorrow," and I roll over and set the phone quietly into place on the bedside table. Cutting the cord.

For that is the bane of a long-distance lover, the knowing that three weeks have passed since I saw her last, and three more will come and go before I see her again.

Tomorrow and tomorrow, and tomorrow. And now it's two weeks until I see her, two weeks until I climb on the plane and fly from sunny California to wintry New York City. We are having a December like no other, 86 degrees, too hot to wear jeans, too hot to wear anything but gauzy, summer-print dresses that skim my hips and thighs, and flit and flirt when I walk.

Too hot to make love? Never.

"The kitchen," I say when it's my turn to call. "On the counter-top."

"The cool tile," she says back, and I know she's with me. "You can watch your reflection in the windows behind me."

I can see it, my green eyes glimmering in the light from the city, while all the lights in the apartment are out. I can feel her arms, the muscles in them, the shift and slide of the muscles beneath her skin. She is holding me tight, and my legs are wrapped just as firmly around her waist. I've got the cock on this time, and I drive it in and out and hard, *hard*, my fingers digging into her arms, my teeth on the ridge of her shoulder, biting to stifle the scream. I work her without a break, like a machine, like a wonderful fucking machine, our parts well-oiled, interlocking, caught in a groove with one destination in sight.

She lifts her hands to the back of my head, cradling me, losing her fingers in the gold foil of my hair. Her kiss is like water, sliding, cool. Her kiss is like the ocean, like I've brought the ocean with me. Her full, cat-mouth on mine is like a dream that makes me sorry to wake up.

Her kiss is like she's with me.

And, in a way, she is.

"Watch us," Giselle says, "Watch the way we move." I peer at our reflection, the black and white tile floor beneath her bare feet, the white marble counter beneath my ass—the reflection of our bodies moving, working, shimmering in the mirror-window.

"You're perfect," I tell her, "Just like that. Keep it going, now. Just like that."

In and out and HARD. Can you feel it? Hard, like a piston, well-oiled, moving up and down, sliding in out. Too good. Too right. I can taste it, oh, god, I can taste it, my hips sliding on the counter, my body working against hers, my hips snapping against hers, too good, too right . . . "Ohhhh!" It's a shriek, louder than I expected, louder than I planned, "Ohhh, my sweet . . . ." and she echoes it back to me, calling out my name, "Stefanie!" as we come together, 3000 miles apart, as we come together and explode.

"Tomorrow," I tell her.

"Tomorrow," she promises.

And tomorrow, and tomorrow, and tomorrow.

It's a week until I see her, and my suitcase is already on the floor, silk skirts and velvet dresses, high heels, jeans, and leather boots. My jacket is back from the cleaners, hanging in plastic from the hook on my door. My lingerie is new, packed in its little compartment, ribbons and lace and fancy things to make her moan. My hair is longer, I think, and it looks different than before, the bangs hanging low over my forehead, the rest a tousled mane that falls past my shoulder blades. I inspect myself as I hope she will— as I know she will—turning in front of the full-length mirror, admiring the lines in my calves, the tone of my thighs, the sleek curves of my waist and breasts.

I imagine her hands on me, her fingers exploring, parting, dipping. I imagine myself through her eyes, and I feel a longing steal over me that is impossible to shake. I lie down on the bed, holding the phone to my chest, wanting to call—but it's too early —wanting her voice to wrap me up and carry me to her.

I press the buttons slowly, the glowing green buttons that mock me somehow, and she answers immediately.

"I want," I start, "Giselle, I want . . ."

"Slower, this time," she says, her voice a lesson in control. "Slower, girl, don't rush it."

"Slower," I breathe back to her, "Okay, all right." Steady now, my fingers probing, steady now, through the soft curtain of my panties. But I can't. "On the floor," I order, my voice strong, my passion winning. "On the floor, Giselle."

And I hear the laugh in her voice, the surprise in her voice, as she says. "Yes, all right. The living room floor."

"I'm on top."

She knows it.

"I'm on top and I'm holding you down."

Oh, yes. She knows it. My hands flat against her shoulders, pinning her to the plush carpet, my knees spread wide at her hips, my body in charge, my will in charge. Faster, I need it faster, and I'm controlling the speed, I'm running this machine.

She arches her fine hips to help me, to give me some leverage. Her hands find my waist and she keeps me steady, keeps that steady, raging beat. Her synthetic cock is a part of me, the hard, throbbing rod, a part of my body. I never release it entirely. I hold it within me and ride it, squeezing it, the contractions running through my body into her, *tight and hard*, release, *tight and hard*, release, her breathing sounds like sobbing to me, her face is flushed with the effort of it, the effort to hold back. She can't, though, because I'm in charge and I don't want her to hold back.

I work her harder, watching her face change. Her curls are matted, her cheeks are covered in a thin sheen of sweat. She's biting her bottom lip as she always does before she comes, and she's moaning, repeating, like a mantra, over and over, "Yes, baby, yes, baby, yes . . ."

I feel it happen inside me, the change inside me, and her fingers dig deeper into my waist, needing to capture me, to hold me to her. I go forward against her, onto her chest, never stopping the pounding rhythm of my hips, faster than ever, faster than anything. She lifts me forward with her hips and we're slamming into each other, slamming like two trains meeting, the crash reverberating through both of our bodies. The crash and then the aftermath of the sparks and fires that shoot through us, every nerve ending tingling, every fiber burning.

She closes her eyes and wraps me in her arms. She holds me to her beating heart and wraps me in her arms. Her voice caresses me, her fingertips soothe me. And it's as if she's here, with me, and not 3000 miles away.

"Tomorrow," she says, the catch still in her voice.

"Tomorrow," I sigh.

And tomorrow and tomorrow and tomorrow.

The plane lands at 6:05. I'm the first one up, the first pushy passenger to the door, and the flight attendant gives me a little "school teacher" frown, as if I should be made to sit down until everyone else has left. But we're grownups here, aren't we? And she can only glower at me while I slide past her with my carry-on suitcase and fly up the enclosed hallway to the gate.

She's right at the front of the greeters. And she has a placard that says, "Stefanie Messinger" in bold black pen and "I Love You," beneath it in red. She's wearing a long navy trench coat still dusted with snow, and she's holding a bouquet of white roses. I'm in her arms before they're fully open to me, snuggling against her chest and bear-hugging her.

"Luggage?" she asks.

"This is it . . . I didn't want to wait."

She grins and takes my hand, leading me to the car park, kissing me while we walk. "Missed you," she sighs, stopping us again and staring into my face. "Missed you so much, Stefanie-girl."

My eyes are wide open, seeing her, and yet I can't really see her. I need to touch her, need the feel of her skin beneath my hands. And I grab her arm tightly and pull her forward. "Giselle," I say, "I want..."

She drives too fast to get me home. She takes all the shortcuts, weaving in and out of traffic, and she drives much too fast. But not fast enough. I snake my hand into her lap while we cruise, I stroke her strap-on firmly through her slacks, longing making my fingers work harder than they should, pressing the molded dildo back against her body—but she sighs and in my mind the bulge there grows.

I lean against her, unbuckling and unzipping and revealing, lean down to take her in my mouth, to take this rigid cock into my mouth and bathe it in sweet, velvety warmth. Her juices have dampened the cock and it tastes of summer, even in this wintery city, she tastes of sinning and heat, like summer, and her cock seems to grow even larger in my throat as I stroke it with my tongue, work it between my lips—though I know this is only an illusion. It seems as if she grows and presses against the back of my throat, and her hand presses against the back of my head, twining her fingers in my hair.

Then she quickly pulls me back and says, "Wait, Stefanie. Wait this time. Go slower this time."

She wants to savor it, and I shiver, regaining my control, and move back in my seat. I stare at her as we drive, memorizing her features, matching them with the image of her in my head. Her golden curls are longer, too, a bit shaggy to the top of her jacket collar. Her eyes are the dark blue of a winter sky at dusk, the clear blue of the water outside my Malibu tower.

I want to devour her, want to dine on her, but I lean back in my seat, set my hand on her thigh, and close my eyes. My heart races, and I mentally try to slow it down. My heart races, and I listen to it beat in my ears. *Slow down*, I whisper, *Slow down*.

We're there: in the garage, in the elevator, in the hallway, in her apartment. We're there: in the living room, in the kitchen, down the hallway, to her bedroom. We're there: stripping—*too quickly, slow it down* —stripping off layers of clothing, watching each other but not helping each other—*off, off, off*—I lose buttons in the process, tearing through my traveling suit, she swears at her shoes, at the knot in the laces of her leather oxfords, and then yanks them off without untying.

On the bed, in her arms, fast, I need her fast. I need her now and hard and fast.

"Shh, baby, slow." Giselle says it, I hear it, but I can't do it.

"I need," I tell her, "I *need*."

And she needs it too, we'll go slow later, we'll go slow after. She turns me on my side and plunges forward, driving inside me, bucking inside me, her eyes open and staring down at me, blue eyes as clear as a midnight sky. Her lips are parted, her teeth clenched, her jaw tight. There's a sheen of sweat on her forehead and the rise of her cheekbones. Her curls are matted, her smell is all around me, her body is all around me. I lose myself in the feeling of her fingers on my breasts, of her warm open mouth on my neck, of her skin against mine. I arch forward, capturing her to me, meeting her lips with my own, drinking in her kisses, drinking in her love.

Our hips snap together, and I open up and take her inside me, draining her with my muscles. She is everywhere at once, pulling out and going down between my legs to taste me there, licking me, lapping at my flood of juices, of nectar, of honey. She turns and I am suckling from her, drinking her as I did in the car, lapping all of my juices away. I work steadier — "keep that rhythm" — then quickly she is up and positioning me on the bed and she is in me from behind, working me and I arch and rock her back. And when I feel it, feel the tremors build inside her, the shudders that work through the muscles of her thighs, I pull away and order her, with just a flick of my hair, with just a look in my eyes, "On the bed

— on your back."

And I'm on her, on top of her, riding, driving, taking her so deep inside me and making that connection happen. Our hearts connecting, our blood rushing at the same beat, at that same crazy beat. Her eyes lock on mine, her hands are in my hair, on my waist, cupping my breasts. Her mouth says, "Kiss me," and I do. Her eyes say, "Love me," and I do. And I do: Love her, kiss her, work her, devour her, *savor* her. Until there is nothing left. Until those waves of power roll over us both and there is nothing left.

In her arms, her smell around me, in her arms with my hair over her shoulders and over my breasts, she says, softly, joking with me, teasing me, "Tomorrow . . ."

And I smile, and I kiss her gently, and I say, "Tonight."

Your Wish is My Command
by N.T. Morley

"I'm not sure I want to do this," said Parker.

"You have got to be fucking kidding me," Vanessa answered, in a pique.

"No," snapped Parker. "I can't do it."

"It was your idea!"

Parker was blushing, but then she'd been blushing for an hour. She looked at her friend hopelessly. Vanessa gave her a look that would have melted chromium steel.

Vanessa's lithe body—raised to well above six feet on the heels of the boots she was wearing—was garbed in a rubber catsuit so tight that it showed every detail of her body. You could even see her nipples through the rubber—though part of that was because the breast cups had sculpted nipples. Vanessa had actually had to shave herself to get into the damn thing, it was so tight, and she'd complained about it endlessly to Parker.

Vanessa was in no mood for a reluctant partner. "You are not backing out of this," she snarled, her face livid with anger. "I am sweating my fucking tits off, Park-ker, and you are not backing out of this, Park-ker!" Vanessa always accentuated both syllables of her best friend's name when she was really pissed off. And she was pissed off with good reason—it *was* Parker's idea to dress up like this for the charity auction. And of course Vanessa was sweating more than Parker—no wonder she was bitchy. "And my fucking feet are killing me—who the hell wears six-inch heels, anyway?"

"Oh, I think they're hot," said Parker nervously, trying to change the subject.

Vanessa responded by tapping the leather riding crop on the inside of her palm a few times—and then whacking it so hard that

Parker jumped. If Parker couldn't manage to weasel out of it, Vanessa was going to do horrible things to Parker's ass—and in front of a hundred screaming frat boys.

Well, they weren't all frat boys, sure. The AIDS charity auction was sponsored by a number of campus fraternities, but it was also sponsored by Lambda House, the campus gay-lesbian organization. A lot of the fraternity brothers had declined to work alongside their more Greek-inclined associates. But some of them had put their prejudices aside and volunteered on the auction, no doubt thinking it would make the chicks think they were "sensitive."

Outside, the booming voice of Big Teddy Gumdrop, DJ at the town's only gay bar, was introducing the act before Parker and Vanessa.

"And now, let's have a big hand for LaKisha Swanson wearing a dress made of condoms!"

There was a round of halfhearted applause as LaKisha strolled out onto the runway. Teddy gushed gloriously about the condom-dress—"Made of *both lubricated and unlubricated* condoms, so you can let those dirty mouths wander—cuts down on time running to the medicine chest!" He got some scattered laughs.

Jesus. A dress made of condoms. That was maybe the only thing Parker could think of that was more humiliating than what she was wearing: A plaid rubber schoolgirl's skirt—micro-mini was understating the matter—and a white latex blouse that hung open, showing her black leather bra. Her hair was up in those goofy pigtails, sticking out obscenely from the top of her head. If they followed the plan—which Parker was trying to figure out some way to avoid—when the announcer called their names they were going to walk out on the runway to the sound of Nine Inch Nails' "Closer," and prance around for thirty seconds before Vanessa forcibly bent Parker over the high stool thoughtfully provided, and whipped the living tar out of her.

Well, that wasn't the idea. It was supposed to be just a couple of whacks, gentle ones, Vanessa had promised. But from the way Vanessa was tapping that riding crop, Parker wasn't entirely sure her best friend wasn't going to go a little overboard. *Maybe a lot overboard*, Parker thought as Vanessa scowled.

"You were the one who came up with this whole idea," said the annoyed Vanessa, as if in answer. "You were the one who thought it would be really fun to dress up like schoolgirl and dominatrix and—"

"Vanessa, I know."

"—go out in front of a million horny frat boys and every fag on the campus and—"

"Vanessa, I know!"

"—lift your skirt and let me spank the shit out of you—all in the name of safer sex, mind you, good clean fun for the betterment of society, something I guess you read in a left-wing sociology textbook—"

"Vanessa! I know!! I know it was my idea! I'm just a little freaked out, is all! Do we have to do the spanking thing?"

"Yes," growled Vanessa. "We have to do the spanking thing. What else are we going to do if I don't spank you?"

"I don't know—dance or something?"

"Dominatrixes and schoolgirls do not dance," said Vanessa primly. "We'll look like fucking crazy Michael Madsen in *Reservoir Dogs*."

"You're a good dancer," said Parker weakly.

"Flattery will get you nowhere."

"Couldn't I just, like, get down on my knees in front of you or something?" The instant Parker had said it, she'd regretted it. Oh, *that* was a fucking bright idea.

To Parker's horror and dismay, Vanessa's face brightened. "Hey, that's a great idea. That would be hot. Total schoolgirl submission thing. The frat boys will love it. You sure you don't mind?"

"I—"

"We're going to have to sit out there for a while when they're auctioning off the outfits anyway—you can just stay on your knees in front of me the whole time! That would be so hot!"

"Oh God, look, I wasn't thinking about that—"

"*Sold! To the gentleman in the pink tux!* Please see the cashier, Pinkie. Ladies and gentlemen—"

Parker felt like a knife had just been jabbed into her guts. She almost doubled over in pain. Her head swam.

"Calm down," whispered Vanessa, her voice cutting through the haze of fear. "Just calm down!"

"Now we have a very special act for you, something I'm sure all you fraternity pledges will drool over! Showing the many faces of latex, we've got—"

"Oh God, oh God, oh God...." Parker just knew she was going to throw up. She just knew it.

"Mistress Vanessa and her slave-girl Parker displaying latex fetishwear from Gothic Dreams!"

As they strolled out onto the runway, they were met with shocked faces, horrified and disgusted at the vileness of Parker's half-naked body and the scandalous nature of her outfit. Frat boys and gay boys alike started screaming and throwing things— popcorn, Calistoga bottles, half-eaten It's-Its—pelting Parker with garbage. Parker felt her stomach seizing up as Vanessa tightened her grip on the leash and a chewed-up Milk Dud it Parker squarely in the tits—

And then Parker puked, heaving the half-digested remnants of pizza and Doritos all over Vanessa. She fell to her knees and started projectile-vomiting into the crowd.

"Parker! Parker! He called our names! We have to go out there."

"What?" Parker was in a daze, still overwhelmed by the thought that her tortured stomach was about to betray her and make her heave her cookies into the crowd.

"It's time. We have to go out there." Then Vanessa leaned close and whispered into Parker's ear: "I'll be gentle."

Maybe it was the warm feeling of Vanessa's breath on Parker's ear. Maybe it was the tender way Vanessa spoke to her—with a feeling of closeness, tenderness, even caretaking. Maybe it was just that in the midst of the vortex of terror she was experiencing, Parker felt so dazed that she let her eyes wander slowly up and down the length of Vanessa's rubber-sheathed body, and realized, for the first time in her life, that her best friend was fucking *hot*.

"Yes, Mistress," Parker heard herself saying, the terror surging up as she curtseyed, the way Vanessa had taught her. "Your wish is my command. I hear and obey."

"Don't be a smart-ass," said Vanessa, and swatted Parker on the ass.

"Here they are!" said Teddy, laughing a little nervously. "Girls, we were beginning to wonder about you — we thought you got started on your act a little early, hah hah hah..."

Parker's head spun at the sudden wave of silence that filled the auditorium as Vanessa led her out onto the stage. Vanessa strolled with power in her gait, her long legs making Parker practically run just to keep up. How the hell did Vanessa walk like that in six-inch heels? Parker was surprised to be struck with the sudden curiosity — maybe Vanessa had had more practice than she let on.

The silence overwhelmed her. Parker felt a wave of fear — they hated her. They despised her. They were disgusted.

Then the cheers started. The sounds washed over Parker and Vanessa as they grew in volume. In a few seconds, Parker's ears were hurting.

Vanessa stepped aside and displayed her schoolgirl, posing with her tits sticking out — sculpted nipples and everything — as Parker curtseyed again, bringing a series of whoops and howls from the crowd. She curtseyed twice more as Teddy spoke.

"That's right, give it up for Mistress Vanessa and Slave Girl Parker. You college kids have it so easy! Back in my day, we *never* had dominatrixes and latex schoolgirls on campus, just acid and ludes!"

The crowd's cheers rose in volume — whether because of the series of curtseys Parker had given or because of Teddy's cheesy drug quip, Parker couldn't say. And she didn't care.

Her eyes were dazzled by the bright lights, but she could see the men and women in the audience howling with laughter, cheering and pointing at her. For an instant she wondered if they were laughing at her or with her, and then she realized that it didn't matter — they were captivated, unable to look away, and that was what mattered.

"Ladies and gentlemen, if there are any of you out there Mistress Vanessa tells me that Slave Girl Parker has been a very, very, very, verrrrrrrrry bad, bad, bad slave girl. Isn't that right, Slave Girl Parker?"

Parker blinked as Teddy shoved the microphone in front of her mouth.

"I said isn't that right, Slave Girl Parker?"

"Y—yes," said Parker nervously. "I've been a bad, bad girl."

On cue, the sound system started playing Fiona Apple's song — like they couldn't have seen that one coming a friggin' mile away, but the crowd erupted in cheers again anyway. Simple minds, simple pleasures.

"And what do we do with bad, bad slave girls, Slave Girl Parker?" giggled Teddy.

"Uhhhhh....." Parker groped for the words.

"We spank the living shit out of them," said Vanessa as she grabbed the microphone from Teddy, her voice low and husky — a voice Parker had never heard from her best friend before. "Isn't that right, Parker?"

Parker put her lips to the already spit-slick microphone, feeling a little creeped out by swapping spit with Big Teddy Gumdrop and her best friend at the same moment. But she managed to say it.

"Yes, Mistress. Your wish is my command."

This time the cheers were so loud they made the microphone feed back.

The riding crop came up, and down again. Parker jumped, but Vanessa was just tapping her shoulder. Vanessa spoke into the microphone: "Then bend over, Slave Girl!"

The crowd went crazy with screams, laughs, and cheers as Parker nervously turned around and then stepped up to the stool that had been arranged for just this purpose. She had known this was coming, but she wasn't prepared for the wave of fear she felt as she slowly bent over, placing her belly above the seat of the stool.

Damn it! She was too tall! She couldn't lean on the stool properly.

"Spread your legs," hissed Vanessa, covering the microphone with her hand — but then the microphone started to feed back. Parker didn't move, so Vanessa spoke into the microphone this time: "Spread your legs, Slave Girl Parker."

Damn it, that's right! They'd tried it with this stool before, and it was too low for her if she kept her legs together. Had she really agreed to fucking spread her legs in front of all these fucking screaming frat boys? She must have been smoking crack. Parker's head spun as she tried to figure out how she could get out of it now.

But she couldn't.

"I said spread your legs, Slave Girl Parker," snapped Vanessa into the microphone. "Are you disobeying your mistress?"

She stuck the microphone into Parker's face, and Parker squeaked "No, Mistress. Your wish is my command."

And then she spread her legs, and the crowd erupted like it hadn't done before.

And Parker spread her legs wider, and snuggled down onto the school, listening as Vanessa gave her the next order.

"Now lift your skirt, Slave Girl Parker."

Oh God, oh God, oh God. She couldn't do that! She was wearing underwear, sure, but what difference did that make? Besides, it was latex underwear — she was sure the crowd would be able to see everything.

"Lift your skirt!"

"Yes, Mistress. Your wish is my command."

Parker's hands were shaking as she reached back and lifted the plaid latex skirt. The crowd howled.

Parker felt more exposed than she had ever been before — because she was. She was standing in front of hundreds of frat boys, legs spread wide, her skirt lifted and only the thinnest, skimpiest latex panties between her and them. Between her vulnerable, exposed body and theirs.

God, what had made her think of that?

At least she wasn't wet. She was much too scared to be wet. Much too freaked out. It was just an act. It was just a game. It had nothing to do with sexual interest. Parker knew she was straight, and besides, even if she hadn't been, Vanessa was, too. And none of these guys would have wanted to fuck Parker anyway.

"Damn!" giggled Teddy. "That's enough to make me straight — almost. Wouldn't you boys like to take that home?"

The crowd erupted again in cheers and shouted encouragements, and Parker realized with horror that she could hear feminine voices among the shouts — "Work it, girl," and "Pussy Power!" in particular.

Parker wondered for the hundredth time how she got into this.

"Are you ready for your spanking, little girl?" Vanessa's voice had a quality to it that Parker didn't recognize — a commanding nature, and a husky sensuality that made her shiver.

"Yes, Mistress. Your wish is my command."

WHACK! Parker jumped at the loud sound — and heard herself screaming.

"If you think that's hard, little girl, wait until you find out what happens when you don't clean up your room!" It was Vanessa, laughing cruelly, sneering down at Parker as the schoolgirl looked over her shoulder at her best friend. But Parker realized that her ass didn't hurt — Vanessa had barely hit her at all. Barely tapped her. She'd just held the microphone so close to Parker's ass that the cropcrack had sounded like a gunshot. How the hell did the crazy bitch think of that trick?

Then she did it again, and even though she knew it was coming, Parker jumped again. The crack rang like a gunshot through the auditorium, and the crowd roared. The microphone whined, and Vanessa put it to her lips again.

"Say 'thank you, Mistress,'" she purred, and Parker felt the microphone against her lips again, slick with spit.

"Thank you, Mistress," Parker heard herself saying, her voice as much a purr as Vanessa's. She couldn't be wet — she was much too freaked out to be wet. Maybe she was just sweating.

"Spread your legs wider, Slave Girl Parker," ordered Vanessa.

Parker hadn't realized that when she'd jumped, she'd snuggled her thighs back together. Without even hesitating for an instant, she spread her legs wide, pulled her skirt up further, and listened to the crowd cheering.

WHACK! She wasn't wet. WHACK! They were all looking at her. WHACK! Looking at her ass, getting hard and wet as they watched her being punished in front of everybody. *In front of everybody. Is Vanessa wet, too? No, no, I'm not wet. I can't be wet. I'm totally straight, and this doesn't even interest me, it's just fun to have all these guys looking at my ass. Fine, then, I'm not wet, but I wonder if Vanessa's wet. She did make that comment once about her boyfriend Todd's Playboy...God, could Vanessa be getting turned on by this?* Parker squirmed and whimpered into the microphone as she felt the barely-there taps on her ass—and found herself wishing, all of a sudden, that Vanessa was hitting her harder. *Not that I'd like that,* thought Parker. *But it would be more realistic. For the crowd, I mean. I wonder what that would feel like? It feels kind of good being hit light like this — I wonder what it would be like to be spanked hard — really, really hard.....*

"One last time," cooed Vanessa into the microphone. "Beg me for it, Slave Girl Parker."

No way, Vanessa couldn't possibly be getting turned on by this. She was just acting for the crowd. Parker's mind was working so fast she almost forgot her line. "Please, Mistress, may I have another?"

Then it happened. Vanessa brought the crop down, hard this time, so hard Parker didn't just jump; she practically screamed. Which was probably more about the fact that Parker had decided, this time, to obediently lift her ass for her mistress' crop, and had done so just as Vanessa brought the crop down. As a result, Vanessa had nailed Parker's pussy dead-on, right between her swollen lips — swollen from heat, of course, being imprisoned in the latex panties, and spread apart only from the tightness of the unbreathing garment, of course—and the pain exploded through Parker's body. Even through the latex panties, it felt like Vanessa had just given Parker a stiff kick from those pointy-toed boots right in Parker's unfortunate cleft.

Vanessa handed Teddy the microphone and leaned close to Parker's face, so close Parker could smell her sweet breath, feel it warm on her face. Could even smell Vanessa's sweat a little—she was sweating as much as Parker was under these hot lights in these latex clothes—and the sharp chemical tang of the latex, like ammonia and condoms mixed together. Parker took a deep breath, scenting her best friend's sweat as she squirmed in pain, shaking her ass to cheers from the audience.

Vanessa's bitch-persona had turned into the worried best friend in an instant — as soon as she realized she'd missed Parker's ass and hit her pussy. "Oh God, sorry, sorry, sorry — oh, I'm so sorry baby, I didn't mean to hit you there — oh, God, are you OK?"

Through stars and whirling pain, Parker felt a trickle of moisture escape the crotch her latex panties and run down her thigh. *They can see it*, she thought as she savored the pain radiating outward from her tortured pussy. *It's just sweat, it's just sweat, it's just sweat, but they think it's something else. It's so hot under these lights, it's so hot inside these panties, I'm sweating. I'm just sweating. I can't believe my whole body isn't pouring sweat. But they think it's not sweat. They think it's something else. They can all see how wet I am—dripping wet, gushing down my thighs. I'm humiliated. I'm totally humiliated, and God, that hurt like a motherfucker. She damaged my pussy. That bitch Vanessa, how dare she do that to me! Why didn't she watch where she was hitting me? Right on the clit—she hit me right on the goddamn pussy. Oh God, I've got to get backstage and masturbate.*

"No," moaned Parker softly into Vanessa's too-close face. "I think I'll be fine."

A horrified look crossed Vanessa's face, as Parker stared into her eyes. She had never really noticed how beautiful her friend was—except in the jealous way that came from Vanessa getting all the guys. But now...it didn't bother her at all.

"Ooooh, that's gotta hurt!" Teddy was laughing. "All right, now that our slave girl's had her spanking, you two just sit there and do your thing while we finish this little bit of business, then you two sizzling-hot girls can go backstage and slide right out of those slutty outfits—hey, there's a thought, now, guys!" The crowd erupted in cheers. "And yes, you naughty boys, you get *these* outfits, fresh off our little sluts' bodies....let's start the bidding!"

Obediently, Parker got off the stool, looked into Vanessa's eyes, saw the fear and discomfort there. Then, what Parker did shocked her. Tenderly, to screams from the crowd that drowned out all previous cheers, Slave Girl Parker stood up on her tiptoes and placed a kiss on her mistress' mouth, not even closing her lips when she felt the full swell of Vanessa's lips against hers, and lingering when she felt the electricity going through her body.

Vanessa didn't kiss back, but she didn't pull away. The crowd's cheers were deafening.

Meekly, Vanessa sat down on the stool, her latex-sheathed thighs pressed tightly together.

And meekly, Parker said "Your wish is my command, Mistress," and lowered herself to her knees and put her head in her best friend's lap.

The two outfits went together for an obscene sum. Some silver-spoon frat boy was going to have a hell of a charge to explain on his father's AmEx next month—"No, really, Dad, it was a charity auction. For.... uh.... starving children in Uganda. Yeah, organized by the Campus AIDS Project."

But not before he and his friends put this outfit to good use, Parker thought wickedly.

After they got backstage, Parker was sure she was going to be able to wait until she got back to her dorm room, but she wasn't. The second she got inside the little backstage bathroom, pulled down her latex panties and sat down on the toilet, she started. She didn't even know she was doing it, really, she just thought how bad she needed to piss and then she was rubbing her clit, feeling her pussy all swollen, sliding one finger down to her pussy between strokes on her clit. Sliding one finger, then two, inside her, discovering only then that she really was wet—wetter than she'd ever been or ever thought she could be—and it wasn't just sweat, though there was plenty of that, too, sheening her whole body under and around the latex schoolgirl's outfit. Sweat dripped from her in steady streams onto the toilet, making a sound not unlike urine dribbling into the bowl.

But what was really embarrassing was that Vanessa wouldn't have suspected anything if the first orgasm hadn't just primed Parker's need for more—and it took her five minutes to come, the second time, rubbing her clit in big circles and leaning back on the toilet so she could work a finger into her pussy. She came so hard she cried out, sounding like a sob, and Vanessa knocked fervently on the door.

"Are you all right?"

"Uh....yeah...." said Parker nervously, her voice shaky as the orgasm echoed inside her body. "I just....I think I'm kind of sick from being so nervous."

"Do you need help? Do you want me to come in?"

Jesus, thought Parker. *Do I ever.*

"No," she sighed. "I'll be out in a minute."

Vanessa needed Parker's help getting out of the catsuit, which had decided to stick to every inch of her skin. Parker even had to unzip the crotch and peel the latex down off Vanessa's ass, and that didn't help matters a bit.

But she didn't say a word, even when she was bent over Vanessa's upthrust buttocks, even when the thought occurred to her that a real slave girl would have shown her submission by licking her mistress' ass in front of that whole auditorium — now what had made her think *that*?

"Pull harder," said Vanessa, and Parker did. The latex suit came free with a wet noise, and Vanessa giggled.

"Our reputation is sealed," said Vanessa miserably, dipping her French fry in ketchup. "We're the sluts of the whole campus. I hadn't expected to attain that honor until my Junior year at least."

"There are worse things, aren't there?" said Parker, lazily toying with a fry.

"And the lesbos. I swear, next time we go to a party, everyone there is going to expect us to make out for them. Nice fucking touch, pervert, kissing me in front of everyone."

"Oh, come on, we didn't do anything they can't see on MTV."

"Yeah, right," snorted Vanessa. "Except we gave it to them live."

"Come on. Guys will be begging us for dates."

A crowd of frat rats came in to the diner, spotted Vanessa and Parker, and recognized them instantly. They started pointing at the two girls and laughing."

"See?" said Vanessa. "They're going to be making fun of us forever. We'll never live this down."

"Come on, we're celebrities. We're peoples' heros."

"Yeah, especially those dykes in the front row."

"So? I think it's pretty cool we had the guts to actually go through with it in front of everybody."

"Oh yeah, right! You're the one who almost chickened out! If I hadn't pushed you out there you'd still be cowering backstage!"

"And I love you for it," said Parker, and Vanessa looked shocked. As if to defuse the loaded statement, Parker grabbed her tits and stuck out her tongue at Vanessa, and the tension dissolved into giggles.

Suddenly, a frat boy appeared at Parker's elbow. Vanessa looked at him angrily.

"You were the girls—"

"Yes," snapped Vanessa meanly. "That was us. What do you want?"

"I was wondering...." the frat boy said, holding out a napkin and a ball-point pen to Parker. "Could I have your autograph?"

Vanessa started laughing hysterically, but Parker didn't think it was very funny. In fact, she thought it was very fucking cool. Which is why Parker just smiled, demurely, looked at the guy—who was hella cute—and said, "Your wish is my command."

She took the napkin and signed her name, while Vanessa laughed her ass off.

Zachary's Needle
by Alison Tyler

"Draw on me, baby," I whisper to Zachary. "Come on, Zach, ink me up."

Zachary stares down at me. His dark green eyes appraise my skin the way any artist assesses a blank canvas. There's a glow to his eyes, a power deep inside them, and I think that he must be picturing the finished product, seeing what the art will look like when it is complete. Then he says, "Breathe, Gina," in a soft, sturdy voice, and I inhale deeply and wait for him to begin.

The waiting—as the song goes—is the hardest part. Waiting and imagining what it will feel like. Pain? Pleasure? Both mixed up together? I've been in this position before, and I should know, but I forget each time as soon as it's over. The way I forget the pain after a bare-bottomed spanking over his lap, or the embarrassment of being taken in public as soon as a scene ends. My short-term memory for situations like that is poor. When the rush of it fades, I'm at a loss. Ready so quickly to try again.

Now, I stare at my lover, impatient. It doesn't make him work faster. Zachary never rushes. He always takes his time as he gets the instruments ready. "It gives the client a final few seconds to reconsider," he told me once. "A last-ditch chance to back out." Of course, I'm not his average client, and I'm not going to back out. Zachary knows that by the time I'm on his table, jeans down or shirt up, naked body part exposed, I'm ready. Still, he offers me the same careful consideration he gives anybody else.

I think crazy thoughts in those quiet moments before the needle bites my skin. Visions like LSD dreams come fast behind my closed lids, and then just as quickly, they burst and fade away. I recall photographs from tattoo magazines, shimmering wings covering one girl's back, a bright red devil's tail sprouting below. Mentally, I categorize the clothes in my closet, deciding which outfits will best expose my latest acquisition—low-slung hip-huggers with a midriff baring top. Perfect....

"Breathe, Gina," Zachary says, letting me know that we're getting closer.

This isn't the most appropriate time to get turned on, but I can't help it. My libido answers to nobody's rules. In those last moments, I give in to my all-time favorite fantasy: Me, sprawled totally nude on a cool vinyl counter at the tattoo parlor. Zachary, with his magic needle, covering every inch of my bare skin with the designs that flicker through his mind. Sprawls and swirls of Klimt-like colors. Dreamscapes that dance when my muscles flex and shift beneath the skin. Butterflies that fly each time I move or stretch or bend.

My vision grows more in-depth. I picture us in our tiny Hollywood apartment afterwards. In the heat and the sweat of our lovemaking, Zachary's firm body slips against mine. He is all lean muscle, long limbs and hard edges, the opposite of my curves, lush breasts, rounded thighs. We go at it ferociously from the start. His strong hands move my hips so that we connect, body to body, the scent of our lovemaking combining in the air.

He is a master at touching me, lifting my body in the air, cradling my ass in his arms. Then he spreads me out on the bed and traces his fingertips over the designs that decorate my skin. His touch electrifies me and I can feel myself growing wetter, sense the pool of liquid sex that starts to spill from between my nether lips. Zachary slides one hand between our bodies to find the true source of my pleasure. He plucks at my slick, wet clit with his thumb and forefinger. Carelessly teasing, tickling, flicking just hard enough to force me to beg for more.

Begging is what I do best.

Finally, he brings his mouth to my cunt, his lips parting, his knowing tongue probing. He drinks from me until I can take it no longer and I come, hard, my hips rising uncontrollably, our bodies are sealed together for one heavenly moment. Then he moves again, slips into a sixty-nine, so that I can suck on his throbbing cock as he continues to dine on me. Zachary gives me no time to recover. It is his mission to make my orgasm stretch out, expand, so that I come and come and come. Climaxing against his mouth is divine, and I tell him so with my body, tell him with my tongue as I trace designs of my own creation up and down his rock-hard pole.

In my mind, while we fuck, the tattoos transfer from my body to Zachary's, from his to mine. Vibrant colors bleed as our two human canvases become one, the artwork merging, spreading, taking shape in new and unusual ways. When we're finished, collapsed and out-of-breath, the once-white sheets draped over our bodies drip with many colors.

"Breathe, Gina," Zachary says again, tearing through my X-rated adventures as a fiery blush rises to my cheeks. If he recognizes my flush, he doesn't let on. His angular face is all business, and I watch as he bends to inspect the fresh skin I have offered up, the best present I could ever give him. Then I shut my eyes, and he moves in closer and presses the silver needle to my skin.

The metal tip is like ice, so cold it if feels hot. I imagine that I can hear each drop of ink as it enters my skin. First, blue—a deep sapphire color like the gem. Then after a few minutes of work, a switch to gold. Pure and powerful, the feel of the colors is transcendent as they meld with my blood, go down deep into my body. Curls of pigment drift on a rich crimson current. Rainbows reflect against the cold white of bones and the dull pink-red of organs.

"*Paint me on the inside,*" I want to tell Zachary. "*Climb inside my body with your magic needle and change the way I look at life. Turn my eyes into stained glass windows. Cover my heart with indelible designs, your name entwined with mine.*"

But he'll just laugh at me. He won't understand. So instead, I say, "Draw on me, baby," in a rich, husky voice that makes him stop working and meet my gaze. I'm his coloring book. I wear his art on my skin, a gallery come to life, a work in progress. "Come on, baby," I say, teasing him, taunting him, "ink me up."

The fine lines around the corners of his eyes crinkle as he smiles. Zachary stares at me for one long beat, and then admonishes me.

"Breathe, Gina," he says.

I do as I'm told. I close my eyes. I take a breath. And I wait for him to color outside of the lines.

About those naughty authors...

Mistress A. ("Blue Denim Pussy") spends a lot of time in dressing rooms. She is currently working on a novel about sex and shopping, her two most favorite naughty passions.

Ann Blakely ("What She Likes...") is the co-author of *The Other Rules: Never Wear Panties on a First Date and Other Tips*. This spoof of the dating guide, *The Rules*, was recently translated into Spanish.

M. Christian ("The House of the Rising Sun") is the author of over 100 published short stories—his work being found in *Best Lesbian Erotica, Best Gay Erotica, Best American Erotica, Best Bisexual Erotica*, and many other books and magazines. He's the editor or co-editor of over nine anthologies, including *The Burning Pen, Guilty Pleasures, and Rough Stuff 1 & 2* (with Simon Sheppard). A collection of his gay men's erotic short stories, *Dirty Words*, is available from Alyson Books—and a collection of his lesbian short stories, *Speaking Parts*, is coming next year (also from Alyson Books). The only thing he likes better than writing is sex.

Becky Chapel ("X-rated Conversations") writes under different names for magazines that, for some unexplained reason, all start with the letter "p": *Playgirl, Parenting, People*, and *Penthouse*.

Sarah Clark ("On Fire") lives and works in Pasadena, California. She writes for several Los Angeles-based entertainment newspapers, doing movie and restaurant reviews and celebrity interviews. Her stories have appeared in anthologies including *Batteries Not Included*.

Dante Davidson ("Appraising Love") is the co-author of the best-selling *Bondage on a Budget* and *Secrets for Great Sex After Fifty* (which he wrote when he was 28). His short stories have also appeared in *Bondage* (Masquerade), in the anthology *Sweet Life* (Cleis), and on the web site www.goodvibes.com.

Lucia Dixon ("Quiet, Quiet") lives a quiet life—at least, it would appear so on the surface. But, as evidenced in her story, you just never know what goes on behind closed doors.... Her work has appeared in *Girls on the Go* and *Gone Is the Shame*.

Shane Fowler ("Focus of Attention") divides her time between Paris and L.A. Under a variety of pen names, her work has appeared in publications including *Best Lesbian Erotica 1996*, *Penthouse Variations*, and *Herotica 4*.

Molly Laster ("Killing the Marabou Slippers") is a well-rounded writer based in Canada. She divides her time between doing the type of writing she likes (erotica) and the type of writing that pays her bills (you don't want to know). Her short stories have also appeared in *Girls on the Go* and *Gone Is the Shame*, both published by Masquerade Books.

Marilyn Jaye Lewis ("Making Whoopie") has written short stories and novellas that have been widely anthologized in the US and UK. Editions Blanche, Paris, will publish the French language edition of her critically acclaimed collection of novellas, *Neptune & Surf*, in Fall 2001. She is coeditor of *The Mammoth Book of Erotic Photography* and recently won Best Erotic Writer of the Year in the UK for 2001. Her upcoming novel, *The Curse of Our Profound Disorder*, was a finalist for The Evans Harrington Award in the William Faulkner Writing Competition in New Orleans. As webmistress, her erotic multimedia sites have won numerous awards. Visit Marilyn's homepage at: www.marilynjayelewis.com.

Elle McCaul ("Trust Me") writes historical romances novels for several different companies. This is her first erotic short story.

Samantha Mallery ("Spring Cleaning") lives on Hilton Head Island, where she teaches golf. Her writing has appeared in the magazines *Zed* and *Eye* and in the anthology *Batteries Not Included*.

Christy Michaels ("Lonesome Highway") has worked as an advertising copywriter, topless waitress, motorcycle messenger, and co-owner of the private club SA-FO. She now lives in San Francisco with her lover and two cats. Her work has appeared in the anthology of lesbian short fiction *Batteries Not Included*.

Beau Morgan ("Dirty Pictures") is a freelance photographer and full-time professor. He has never stopped his search for the perfect model.

Julia Moore ("Pinch the Head") is the co-author of the best-selling book *The Other Rules* (Masquerade, 1998), a spoof of the insane dating guide *The Rules*. Her erotic short stories have appeared in *Sweet Life* (Cleis) and on the web site www.goodvibes.com

N.T. Morley ("Your Wish is My Command") is the author of such erotic novels as *The Parlor*, *The Castle*, *The Limousine*, *The Library*, *The Circle*, and *The Office*, published by Masquerade Books. A new Morley novel will be published in 2001 by HG Orion Publications.

Isabelle Nathe ("Games People Play") has written for anthologies including *Come Quickly for Girls on the Go* (Rosebud), and *A Century of Lesbian Erotica* (Masquerade). Her work has appeared on the web site www.goodvibes.com.

Lisa Pacheco ("Joining the Club") dedicates her story to all of the creative people who like to play in public.

Emilie Paris ("Underwater") is a writer and editor. Her first novel, *Valentine*, (Blue Moon) is available on audiotape by Passion Press. She abridged the 17th century novel, *The Carnal Prayer Mat* for Passion Press, which won a Publisher's Weekly best audio award in the "Sexcapades" category.

J. Richards ("In Progress") works at a production company in Los Angeles and is currently co-writing a screenplay about the Internet.

Thomas Roche ("Curtain Call") is the editor of the *Noirotica* series, which consists of four volumes currently being published and reprinted by San Francisco's Black Books. His short stories have appeared in more than 100 magazines and anthologies, and he has written more than 200 nonfiction articles for print and online publication, mostly on the topics of sex, death, rock & roll, mystery fiction, organized crime, and espionage. Some of his stories are collected in his book *Dark Matter*. His anthology *Best Men's Erotica* collects erotic writing by men, and will be published in 2002 by Cleis Press.

Alison Tyler ("Zachary's Needle") is a naughty girl. With best-friend Dante Davidson, she is the co-editor of the best-selling collection of short-stories *Bondage on a Budget*. Her short stories have appeared in anthologies including *Erotic Travel Tales* (Cleis), *Noirotica 3 & 4* (Black Books), *Wicked Words 4, 5 & 6* (Black Lace), *Guilty Pleasures* (Black Books), *Best Women's Erotica* 2002 (Cleis), and *Sweet Life* (Cleis). Her recent novels include *Learning to Love It*, *Strictly Confidential*, *Sweet Thing*, and *Sticky Fingers*, all published by Black Lace. Look for her short stories on www.goodvibes.com and on www.tinynibbles.com.

Mary Jo Vaughan ("Vulcan Mindblower") has written stories for *Girls on the Go* (Masquerade), *Batteries Not Included* (Diva), and *Bondage on a Budget, Volume II* (Pretty Things Press). She's always anxious to try a new drink.

Craig T. Vaughn ("Nobody's Business") is a musician living the Hollywood lifestyle in L.A. His work has appeared in a wide variety of music 'zines. Look for him hanging out at Kings Road Café or Swingers—but not before noon.

Eric Williams ("Roger's Fault") has written for anthologies including *Sweet Life* (Cleis), *Best Men's Erotica* (Cleis), and *Bondage on a Budget, Volume II* (Pretty Things Press).

Gabriella Wise ("Erotic Explorations") spends a lot of time in bed. You know, doing "research." Her short stories have appeared on www.tinynibbles.com.

Bonus Chapter!
Excerpt from
*Naughty Stories from A to Z,
Volume II*

The Sex Test
by Alison Tyler

My best friend Roxanne and I share everything, from secrets to lipstick to the occasional man. Years ago, we had keys made to each other's apartments, for those fashion emergencies when she desperately needs to borrow one of my leather jackets and I'm out of town. Or the occasions when I want to lift one of her treasured Led Zeppelin LPs and she doesn't answer her page. We lend, give, and trade items all the time. So when she brought over a stack of magazines that she'd finished reading, I thought nothing of it.

Looking back now, there *was* something odd about the way she handed the magazines to me. A subtle rosy blush colored her normally pale, freckled skin. A strangely charged heat shone in her dark green eyes, and she ducked her head rather than staring at me straight on. "Don't worry about giving them back, Jodie," she told me. "I'm finished."

I hefted the stack, then fanned out the top few, looking them over. She had all the girly genres covered—a gossip rag, a fancy foreign number, and a famous one devoted to helping women transform themselves for men.

"They're just fluff," she continued, sounding somewhat embarrassed. But then, as if she couldn't help herself, she added, "Who knows, maybe you'll learn something." She motioned with a casual nod to my faded Levis, long-sleeved white Tshirt, and battered boots. I'm no gambler when it comes to my wardrobe. I like the clean lines of jeans and a tank top, the soft caress of well-worn leather, or a sharp-looking suit when I need to dress up.

Roxy's the opposite. We are both long and lean, but my best friend tends to dress more exotically, choosing splashier colors, tighter fits. She's gone through all of the trendy phases—punk, femme, even the military look that was the rage again this year. Her spunky attitude takes her through even the most outrageous fad, and sometimes I've actually been tempted to join her on a fashion adventure. Nobody but Roxy could get me to trip along after her in a pair of dangerous high heels instead of my normal Doc Martins, but she's done it. No one but my best friend could cajole me into wearing a bright lipstick red sarong at the beach, and Roxy's done that, too.

"Have fun," she grinned, watching as I set the magazines on my glass coffee table. "I'll call you tomorrow." Then she kissed me goodbye, trailing her fingertips through my shoulder-length brown hair, holding me close so that I could smell the perfume of her skin. Yes, we give each other bear hugs and friendly kisses all the time, but this embrace was filled with a little more longing than a regular goodbye smooch. I stared after her, wondering exactly what was going on, but not able to guess.

After she left, I got comfortable on the white leather sofa in my living room, perusing the various magazines in the fading summer sunlight. Outside my open window, I could hear the sounds of happy voices overlapping, couples giggling together on the gold-flecked sands of the Santa Monica Beach. By myself that Friday evening, I was thrilled to have such mindless reading matter to fill my time. It would keep my thoughts away from the fact that I was dateless.

The first magazine was a slim volume filled with gossip about celebrities I didn't know. I flipped through it in no time. The second, a slick European edition, took me longer. I daydreamed my way through the 400-plus pages of the spring fashion bonanza, pictured myself in the different designer suits, tried to imagine which pieces would look better on me and which would be more flattering to Roxanne. Not difficult at all. She'd wear the beaded ball gowns, the fantastic, frilly confections made of fluttering lace. I'd accompany her in the sleek black suits, the wide-legged crepe de chine pants, the butter-soft black leather.

By the time I'd visualized each of us in all of the different outfits, it was getting late, and I decided to move to my bedroom. First, I poured myself a glass of chilled white wine, then changed into a black tank top and a pair of gray silk boxers. In my bed, I slid beneath the covers and reached for magazine number three. This was a famous one, known for articles filled with sexual ideas, innuendos, and reader confessions. I consider it the equivalent of eating some brightly colored, lip-staining drugstore candy made entirely of synthetic ingredients. Not good for you, but oh so sweet going down.

I worked my way through slowly, as if reading about an alien culture. As I flipped the shiny pages, I learned the proper way to wear sheer pink lip gloss (as if I'd ever give up my trademark hue of deep, true crimson), read the amazing statement that "navy blue is the new black"—I still don't get that—before finally coming to a quiz in the very center of the magazine. "How Much of a Risk Taker Are You Beneath the Sheets?" The headline queried. Below, was the interesting subhead: "What Your Secret Fantasies Reveal About You."

Well, I'm not a risk taker at all. I didn't need a stupid quiz to tell me that. I'm the type to weigh my options, dipping my toes in the shallow end to test the temperature first. It takes a while for me to make decisions, and once I do, my mind is set. But before I could simply turn the page and move on, I noticed that Roxanne had already filled out the questionnaire. She'd used a fine red pen, circling the different letters of the multiple choice answers. I wondered whether I would be able to guess the way she would respond to each query. That was the *real* test.

Still, I hesitated for a moment before starting. Would she want me to know her innermost fantasies? That was easy to answer: Roxanne and I tell each other everything. This would simply be a fun way for me to exercise my brain power, trying to guess how she would fill in a silly sex test.

The first question jumped right into the subject matter: *Choose the fantasy that most describes your hidden desire. A) Taking the upper hand in a bedroom situation. B) Sharing the power with a partner. C) Letting your lover set the stage.*

C was circled twice.

Hmmm. That one took me by surprise. My instincts told me that she'd have chosen A, for sure. Roxanne has the type of firecracker personality that often accompanies bright red hair and golden-freckled skin. I'd assumed that she would be the one on top in any situation—between the sheets or otherwise. With a bit more interest, I read on.

Question two asked the test-taker to put the following fantasies in order, with the one that was the most arousing at the top.

Role playing
Exhibitionism
Voyeurism
Food play
Bondage

Roxanne hadn't bothered ranking them at all, as if the concept didn't interest her in the slightest. Instead, underneath the different choices, she'd written in the indecipherable statement: *Being found out.*

Now what did that mean—and why would it be a turn-on?

I took another sip of wine, considered calling her and asking her about her answers, and then decided to simply keep on reading. This was the most exciting stuff I'd found all night.

The next part of the quiz was made of several phrases, requiring the reader to mark a T for True or F for False. *I have participated in the following activities:*

• *Played with sex toys*
• *Acted out role-playing fantasies*
• *Tried a menage a trois*
• *Experienced with bondage*
• *Been with another woman*

Each statement had a "T" next to it, and the final one had an exclamation point written in by hand. From sharing stories in the past, I knew that Roxanne was in no way a tentative lover. She'd told me about the time she'd taken her thong off in the window of a cafe on Main Street. Without thoughts of reprisals, she'd spread her slim legs so that her date would be able to see her pantyless pussy when he returned from feeding the meter. He'd paid the check immediately, hurrying her out behind the restaurant for a bit of public sex in the parking lot, so excited that he couldn't even wait until they got home. Which was exactly what Roxanne had been hoping for.

Then there was the lover who'd liked to dress her up. They'd often enjoyed decadent fantasies come to life in the guise of a headmistress and naughty pupil, or kinky nurse and shy patient. She had thrown herself into the fun of make-believe, dragging me along with her to thrift stores on Melrose in search of the perfect costumes.

"I need a cheerleader skirt," she'd confessed. "Something short and pleated."

We'd spent hours perusing the racks at all of our favorite haunts until she'd come up with the perfect red and white pleated number. "Dan's going to flip when he sees this," she'd said, pleased, before correcting herself. "Well, I'm actually the one who's going to flip for him, and he's going to come from watching." She did a mock cheer to show me exactly what she meant.

Roxanne never seemed to feel awkward talking about sex with me. She'd even called me late, late one night, needing to immediately share an encounter she'd had with two of her co-workers. After a day-long, stressful meeting at the ad agency, the threesome had gone out drinking to one of Roxanne's favorite watering holes.

It was that season when brushfires plagued this most wealthy of communities, and from the bar located on the top floor of a hotel, they had watched Malibu burning. Something about witnessing the destruction of all that valuable real estate had made Roxy hot. She'd found the nerve to come on to both of the handsome and receptive co-workers. They'd paid for their margaritas and then gotten a room in the hotel. There, these lucky men had spent several hours making her sexual sandwich fantasy come true, with Roxy in between as the filling.

But somehow even knowing all of these stories from her past, I'd never have guessed that she'd been with a girl. Or that she'd tried any sort of bondage. I couldn't envision her captured, her wild, untamed spirit reined in. Where had I been? Had she tried to tell me but felt that I wasn't willing to hear?

I was anxious to find out what else I'd missed hearing about. Yet another stab of guilt at reading the quiz stopped me. How would I feel if Roxy had stumbled on my own filled-in questionnaire? That was an easy question to answer: I'd never take an idiotic test like this, wouldn't think to waste my time on one. If I had, though, I definitely wouldn't mind Roxy reading my answers. There was nothing about me that she didn't know already. So taking another sip of wine, I quickly got over my moral issues and plunged on.

Question four focused on dirty movies. Next to the titles were brief write-ups, in case the questionee hadn't seen the flick. I'd seen them all. And I knew Roxanne had, as well.

Which erotic movie would you most easily see yourself starring in:
- *Basic Instinct (Dominant woman)*
- *9 1/2 Weeks (Submissive woman)*
- *Bound (Lesbian relationship)*

The second and the third titles were underlined, letting me know that she wanted to try a submissive role in a girl-girl relationship. And suddenly instead of simply acting like a private detective, peeking into my friend's hidden fantasy life, I found myself getting aroused.

Oh, Roxanne, I thought. *You naughty, naughty girl.*

Now, the way she'd acted earlier in the evening made sense to me. She'd been revealing herself in an unexpected manner. Carefully, cautiously. And that wasn't like my Roxanne at all. A born risk taker, she was used to spelling things out clearly from the start. With any other potential lover, she'd have been bold and outspoken. Not with me. The lengths she'd gone through to get into my mind were both surprising and flattering. How she'd bookended the magazine between the others, using them as merely innocent props, knowing that I'd reach for this one later in the night, guessing easily my routine of climbing into bed to enjoy the frivolous volume.

Oh, Roxanne, I thought again. *You aced that quiz, didn't you? You're the number one risk taker of all. Go to the front of the class, girl.*

But what did it all mean? She was coming on to me. That was for sure. Yet why hadn't we gone this route before? She knows full well that I like both men and women, and she also knows that I play the top role whenever I can. My personality may not be that of a standard risk-taker, for I am methodical in my dealings. From my work to my social life, I enjoy order, calm, and the power of being in charge. It floods through me in a rush, from my very center outward to the edges of my body. Bringing someone else to that highest point of pleasure, being in charge of their fulfillment, that's what makes me cream. If submitting is a turn-on for a lover, it works well with my need for dominance.

Sprawling back against the pillows, I slid a hand under my nightshirt, finding the waistband of my charcoal silk boxers and then stroking myself lazily through the material. My thoughts were entirely of Roxanne, of me and Roxanne, playing the way she obviously wanted to play.

In my fantasy, I saw Roxanne letting go. Tied, or cuffed, to my bed, her supple body trembling, her head turning back and forth on my pillow, that long glossy hair of hers spread in a fiery mane against my white sheets. And I saw myself, not undressed yet, still wearing a pair of my favorite faded jeans, a tight white tank top that perfectly fit my lean, hard-boned physique, and holding something in my hand. Closed my eyes tighter, as if that would make the image come clearer to me. Ah, yes, it was a crop, and I was tracing the tip of the beautiful weapon along her ribs, down the basin of her concave belly. A belly I've admired so many times in dressing rooms, or out at the beach, although never have I let my fantasies get away from me.

Now, I did, seeing it my mind as I parted her pretty pussy lips and sliding the braided edge of the crop up inside her, getting it nice and wet.

My hand pushed my boxers aside, needing direct finger-to-clit contact. Slowly, but firmly, I made dreamy circles around and around. And I thought about Roxanne's tongue there, working me when I finally joined her on the bed. She'd still be tied. Bound to my silver metal bed frame. But her tongue would be free to act how it wanted to. I'd bring my hips in front of her, use my own fingers to part my nether lips, let her get a good look at me inside before allowing her to kiss my cunt.

When she was ready, and I was dripping, I would press myself against her face, would let her tongue-fuck me until I could hardly take the pleasure. Only then would I turn around, slide into a sixty-nine, rewarding her with the present of a well-earned orgasm. I'd eat her until her whole body trembled, slip my tongue up inside her, paint invisible pictures on the inner walls of her pussy—

With a harsh intake of breath, I stopped. Stopped touching myself. Stopped fantasizing. What if I was wrong? Maybe she had simply filled out the quiz for the hell of it, had forgotten all about it and given the magazine to me in total innocence. What if I was the one reading things into this, making the wrong assumptions? Yes, it looked as if we'd be perfectly matched in the bedroom, but perhaps that wasn't what Roxanne had in mind at all. Hell, maybe she hadn't even been the one to take the quiz.

Feeling an unexpected sense of panic burst through me, I reached for the magazine again, skimming the remaining questions for signs that Roxanne was the test-taker, and that she'd been answering the queries for my eyes only. It didn't take me long to find the proof I needed. There, as usual, at the end of the quiz, were the directions for tallying the results, followed by three different write-ups explaining the scores: Cool-headed vixen, Hot-blooded mama, and Bungee-jumping bad-ass babe.

A heavily-handed X had been drawn fiercely through the three different writeups, and Roxanne had inserted a new one in her careful handwriting in the margin. It said, "Frisky Femme Feline: Loves her friends, and loves to take risks, but sometimes doesn't have the guts to say what she wants. Which is this: You. I want you, Jodie. Call me and let me know if you will play the way I like. Will you?

Would I?

Now, it was my turn to forget my careful, plodding manner, my style of weighing all facts and figures before making a decision.

Roxanne's cell number is programmed into my phone's memory, and I reached for the handset and pressed one key on my speed dial. Maybe she wouldn't answer—she'd said she had plans for the night—but I'd leave a message.

I didn't have to. She answered on the very first ring, as if she'd been waiting for my call.

"It's me," I told her.

"Hey, Jodie," she said, her voice ultra-casual. She didn't know if I'd read the test. That was obvious from her tone.

"Where are you?"

"Why?" she asked, still playing the innocent.

"How soon can you be here?"

Now, I heard her laughing, relief in the quickness and ferocity of her giggles, and then I heard another noise that made my heart race. The front bell. She was right outside. A risk-taker to the very end. Risking her heart. Putting herself out for potential embarrassment, but probable pleasure.

Tossing the phone on the bed, I hurried to the front door, just as she let herself in with her spare key. Through the open doorway, I saw from the scattering of cigarette butts that she'd been sitting outside on my front porch the whole time, waiting, hoping. The thought that she'd pictured me reading her fantasies turned me on even more than I already was. What would she have done if she'd known that I was touching myself while dreaming about her?

"Get inside," I said, motioning with my head toward the bedroom. But we didn't make it that far. We couldn't. Roxanne and I only had the patience to shut the door, to stop in the center of my living room and reach for each other. My hands worked quickly to undress her. Hers helped me as we got her white peasant blouse over her head, pulled down her faded cut-offs, revealed the wonder of her body as she kicked out of the navy lace thong she had beneath.

"Navy's the new black," I muttered as I pulled my clothes off.

She gave me a quizzical look, but didn't speak.

"That's one of the things I learned from your magazines."

As I spoke, I pushed her back against the leather sofa, making her knees bend as she sat on the lip of it. I took my spot on the floor in front of her. Unlike the cool quality of my fantasy, the steely way in which I held out her pleasure until the end, I needed my mouth on her pussy immediately, needed her taste on my tongue, her sweet, tangy juices spread over my skin. Slow and steady, as always, I worked her. She was divine, sublime, her creamy nectar like nothing I'd ever tasted before. The way she moved, her hips sliding forward, her hands lost in my hair. Every touch, every moan let me know how right we were together.

Now, that we were really in synch, I found that I could start to relax. Roxy was almost desperate, yearning, wanting me to let her climax. I decided I would, if she could answer my questions. Lifting my lips away from her sex, I started off.

"A) You want my mouth against your pussy—"

"Oh, yes."

"Let me finish," I admonished her, and when I looked up into her eyes, I saw that she was paying me careful attention. "A) you want my mouth against your pussy, or B) you want to roll over on your stomach and let me play back there."

Roxy sighed hard, understanding what I was offering, and she answered by moving her body, rolling onto her stomach and pressing her face against the smooth surface of my leather sofa. Quickly, I parted her rear cheeks, touching her hole with my tongue. Just a touch, but I felt the electrifying shudder that slammed through her body. Roxy, my bad girl, loves to be explored like that—she'd told me so once when we'd stayed out all night drinking. Confessed exactly how much she liked it when a lover teased her between her heart-shaped cheeks.

My fingers slid under her hips and up in her snatch, my tongue probed and played. I ate her from behind for several minutes, and when I was ready to move on, I leaned back and asked question number two.

"You planted the test where I could find it—"

Again she interrupted me, sighing the word, "Yes," as if it were an entire sentence. "Yessssss."

"Not finished, baby," I told her, and she shook her head, as if she knew she'd done something wrong. I could tell that she was dazed by the proximity of her orgasm, and that was exactly why I wanted to keep teasing her. My main talent in bed is the ability to hold off. To force myself to wait for that final release, and to help my lovers wait for it, as well. Anticipation is my favorite aphrodisiac.

"You planted the test where I could find it—" I said again, watching as Roxy, with her head turned to the side, bit her bottom lip to keep herself from responding too early. "Rather than simply telling me what you wanted because you thought that I might punish you for playing dirty."

"Oh, true," Roxanne purred. "True, Jodie. True."

That was all I needed to hear. I brought one hand against her ripe, lovely bottom, spanking her hard on her right cheek, then giving her a matching blow on the left. Roxanne sucked in her breath, but didn't move, didn't squirm or try to get away. How pretty my handprints looked against her pale skin. I wanted to further decorate her, but I couldn't keep myself from parting her cheeks again and kissing her between. Roxanne could hardly contain herself now. The spark of pain mixed with the pleasure confused and excited her, and she ground her hips against the edge of my sofa, wordlessly begging for something. For more.

I gave her more. Alternating stinging, sharp spanks with sweet, French kisses to both her ass and her pussy, sliding my mouth down along her most tender, private regions, pushing her further toward the limits of her pleasure.

Then, once again, I stopped all contact, sensing exactly the right moment to ask the final question on my own, personal Sex Test. "You're about to come on my tongue," I said my mouth a sliver away from her skin just before I brought her to climax. "True or false?"

"Yes, Jodie," she whispered as the pleasure rose within her. "True—"She dragged out the word, as if it meant something else.

I brought her to the limits, and then was silent after that. There were no questions left to ask. Only answers, given silently by her body, and by my own.

Pretty Things Press

Naughty Stories
From A to Z

Bondage on
a Budget

Naughty Stories
From A to Z—Volume

30 Erotic Tales
Written Just For Him

30 Erotic Tales
Written Just For Her

Bad Girl

www.prettythingspress.com